count me gone

. . . .

Annabel and Edgar Johnson

SIMON AND SCHUSTER • NEW YORK

Fourth Printing

SBN 671–65006–8 Trade
SBN 671–65007–6 Library

Library of Congress Catalog Card Number: 68–16147
Manufactured in the United States of America
by The Book Press Incorporated
Designed by Betty Crumley

For Ann and Jake

COUNT ME GONE

foreword

. . . .

The tangled metal had once been a blue coupe.
Now it lay in the weeds like a new kind of sculpture,
dangling a chrome manifold. In the sultry summer
night came the faint crackle of a police radio. The
patrol car, parked back along the highway, sent
down a beam of light to the spot where two officers
crouched beside a boy.

Thrown clear, he was stretched under the sumac
bushes that had broken his fall. His eyes were half
open, but the lanky body was limp, held together by
tight pants and a T-shirt.

Another patrolman came down off the shoulder

of the road with a steel tape. "Seventy-one feet from lift-off to first point of impact; must've been doing ninety or better. Is he conscious?"

"In shock, it looks like. Can you hear me, fellow, what happened—asleep at the wheel?"

A slight shake of the head—sun-streaked hair, long behind the ears.

"You been smoking grass?"

"No, sir." The answer came from a long way off.

"Driver's license in order—name, Rion Fletcher. Age, eighteen. O.K., son, try to remember—was it the lights from the oncoming traffic that confused you?"

"What traffic?" He looked up vaguely at the night bugs swarming in the beam of the spot. "Very simple . . . got going too fast, couldn't make the curve."

A swift look shuttled between the law officers. "Take it easy, kid, ambulance is on the way." They didn't mention that this stretch of highway is straight as a rifle shot.

It was not until three days later that Rion found out—from a lawyer, who walked into the private room at the hospital where the boy lay askew, as if he'd been fighting the bed sheets, the tape on his ribs, the rough-dried hospital gown. With his head dug back against the pillow, he measured his visitor with a restless look.

The attorney, a man of tired hair and cluttered face, full of eyebrows and bifocals and sharp blue eyes behind the glasses, met the stare with offhand courtesy as he introduced himself.

It made the boy squirm and thrust at the sheets in a gesture of protest. "I've got my folks coming around, not even listening to me. And these nurses sticking the needle—I've got doctors all over me. Listen, sir, I'm sorry, but I don't feel like it."

"Your parents hoped you'd talk to me, Rion. Lawyers, like bartenders, are professional listeners."

"They already made up their mind—my folks. They decided I'm nuts."

"You can hardly blame them for being confused. They come home from a vacation to find you facing charges of assault, resisting arrest, striking an officer, unlawful flight, reckless driving—"

"So I plead guilty. I know it turns them rigid. Nobody in our family ever went to jail before. But I'm the one getting busted and I'd rather, than be tagged for a kook. So if they sent you here to rig up some case that I was temporarily off my rocker, please count me out."

The attorney studied the young face, the nervous flick of stubby blond lashes, and sat down. "For the record, I don't rig anything for anybody. Look, son, I'm on your side. But there are things which need explaining, this odd lot of charges and an incredibly wild bit of driving—"

"What's wild? It could happen to anybody— you're in a hurry to get gone, it's night, all at once you're fighting a curve."

The lawyer had been waiting for it—his voice toughened slightly. "Never try to con your own counsel, Rion. There was no curve."

"What do you mean, that highway was coming at me like a roller coaster."

"No curve, no skid marks. Your wheels hit the shoulder square—you apparently didn't even try to stop. Since there was no evidence of drugs in the lab tests, the only theory anyone can offer is that you panicked, you were running from the law too hard. Or that you gave up running, as of the moment you wrenched the wheel over."

The silence in the room was stirred by the rattle of the air conditioner, the hushed noises from the corridor outside. At last the boy said, "So that's it— why these doctors keep hammering on my knee. Asking am I depressed, they think I pulled that spin-out on purpose. That's why the folks keep wanting to sock me away for a long rest in the freak farm. Listen, can they do it? Don't I have some civil rights?"

"A few, but it takes an attorney to file sharp edges on them. And I can't, unless you level with me."

"No curve . . ." The loosely assorted limbs under the sheets grew still and helpless. He gave the lawyer a glance that steadied into a look of resignation. "I guess I'll have to spill it. Only tell me one thing— my brother, Doug. When I ask about him, the folks just shuffle their ankles. Have you seen him? Has he said anything?"

"Your parents did mention an older brother— they didn't say he was concerned in this."

"Good Lord. If it was only jail, I swear I'd let 'em throw the book. But when your own folks start thinking you've really flipped your lid—like I said, they don't want to listen. It's not their fault, but if I start to tell them even a little of it, they say I'm not well, I better rest. Maybe you can put it so they'll understand. When you know the whole works, I mean. If you've got that much time—?"

"Take it from the top, son. Say, when you got fired from that summer camp job. I understand you gave in to some curious impulse—when was it, a week ago Sunday? Fill me in about that."

1

· · · · · · · · · ·

What it was, I got slightly lost. Seemed like a real swinging idea, I'd have been O.K. when the sun came up. Why everybody should worry? The most interesting thing I bet ever happened at that camp. But they scream, I got lost in the woods!

By then it was 3 A.M. Sunday morning—the director *had* to fire me. Of course, I think he's got no guts, but you can't blame somebody for that. Look, sir, I don't want to say anything against the place. I should've stuck to teaching the kids baseball.

That's what I was hired for, they told Pop they needed somebody quick. And I only went along with it because I'd just graduated from high last June, which was another mistake. This whole year I kept getting ready to flunk out. So when you skid through, all at once I needed to think—which is the wrong thing for a summer camp.

Take these other goofball instructors—you mention some question, "Well, what *are* you going to do with the whole rest of your life?" They vote you the earth's hairiest creep, very funny. I told them, "Who says? You don't look like *you* crawled out of any ruts." Me, if I stop trying stuff out I'm dead, what's the difference.

So it was a good thing I got fired. I told them, send my junk home if they felt like it, I couldn't care less. All I wanted was to peel off out of there. No, we weren't allowed to have our cars, I just pointed myself north and began to shank it.

Maybe it sounds weird, but the minute that director said, "You're finished," I began to feel good. All the old tangle slipping away, I never felt that good in my life. Down in those hills, walking along, it loosens you up—I kept thinking, "Boy, you're on your way." You'd think it was just that easy, too, at least about five in the morning. You know how things fade in on TV when all the leaves get sharp?

Some girl could've come through the fog and handed me a bar of soap, I wouldn't blink. It even smelled like that. Like the ideas were out there all around, dripping off the trees. Just name it, I'll do it!

No, Lord no, I didn't have anything in mind. It was more like: get with it, boy, you're never going to be in better shape. Everybody gets set up when they leave high, I guess, wanting to be something. And when the sun came up, it all seemed so clear, everything filtered. I even thought, college—well, it's not impossible, why not?

Forget I mentioned it. It's just that my brother, Doug, got his degree. Only a couple of months ago, and I never heard anybody ask him something he couldn't answer. Take me, if there's some question I don't know, I always said, "I don't know." F, just like that—I never seemed to wise up.

Doug's practically brilliant, anybody mentions a subject he's got it cornered right now. I don't mean he's the mouthy type, he's got a lot of charm like my mother. They say he favors her, while I've got Pop's cheekbones and long legs.

So I was on the move, with all that quiet—I thought, now's the time to step out big. Things were beginning to come in on me.

But about then somebody pulls up and says, "Climb in." I shouldn't have done it. He notices my baseball cap and starts gabbing along, about the Washington Senators aren't going to be in the cellar this year, no sirree, not this year. I guess he was from the East, he wouldn't shut up once all the way back to the city.

Also it got me there in the hottest part of the afternoon, and he dropped me off about thirty blocks from the house. I was hurrying—it's no good trying to think, once you're back in town. All I wanted was to get home under a cold shower and sack out for a while—I hadn't done any sleeping since a couple of nights ago. Or longer—I'd been all edges lately. So I thought Doug and me would batch around—goof off and not shave and drink some beer and leave the dishes in the sink, we'd talk. I should mention, the folks were on this cruise, and they gave the maid her vacation, too.

So the minute I stepped in the front door. I thought, who needs flowers? It smelled like a funeral going on, chilly and dim. I stood there in the hallway—they were florist-type flowers—and me without even a shower for two days. I don't know why I thought of that except my beard is coming on like a brass brush this year. And when I walked into the living room, there's this girl sitting. Me, all sweaty and hot—I don't know, she made me sore.

Not too bad-looking, but she wasn't great, either. She was there, that's all. A hundred percent there. I think she had on a white suit. And these shoes with the pointed toes, it makes you sick what it must do to their feet. Long dark hair, like she hung it out to dry—college types, they all think they're folk singers or something.

Doug is staring at me like he got an olive stuck in his eye. His crew cut is practically rigid. He wears it short, he thinks I let mine get pretty uncouth—which I do. I know I wasn't much of a great sight to see, but I couldn't figure why he was all that shook. If he wants to ask a girl over, he's got his driver's license.

Of course he comes out of the freeze fast, introducing everybody. He tells me her name's Shirli with an "i" and she's visiting an aunt here in town, which can be very phony. Oh, I guess she could have an aunt. With that Cleopatra-type jewelry, and the way she lit a cigarette. But there was something odd, I don't know, her knees or something.

That's one thing Doug and me never did bull about much. I've no idea how he makes out with women, he's the type that would rather not discuss it. He doesn't even care for you to come in when he's taking a shower. He never said so, but you can tell. That's why it seemed to me she wasn't exactly his spoonful.

Just the way she sat, with her shoulders sort of split-level, giving me this little well-well smile.

So I wanted them to know I wasn't going to get in the way. "Don't mind me, I'm just drifting through," I said. "See you around."

"Don't let me run you off," she says, if there's any kind of remark I hate. "There are already too many drifters in the world."

Doug does a quick take on that. He knows he ought to show an interest in me, but right now it's hard. "Sure, old buddy, stick around. Didn't expect to see you home for a month yet. What's up? Time off for good behavior?" He sounded like he was nervous.

I told him, "I escaped. Through a hole in the woods, and I need about three days' sleep, so excuse me if I go hit the pillow. Have fun, everybody."

This Shirli is still nailing me with the smile. "When you tire of your lonely bed, come down and let us revive you with food and drink and wild laughter." Turns out she's staying for supper.

"No thanks," I told her, "I can take care of my own survival."

For some reason that slayed her—she has this kind of laugh, you don't know whether she might start crying instead. And all of a sudden, I didn't care too much about being the floor show—it was flattening Doug a little. So I'm on the move when she calls after me.

"Oh-Rion—" She means this constellation, people

are always kidding me about my name. "We'll be looking for you to rise early in the evening."

I went on up to my room. I thought, what difference—so he's got a date tonight. But I guess that wasn't what I was really thinking. I mean—dog-gone, I don't like this.

. . . .

For the first time since they had carried him into this sanitized room, Rion felt the world swinging back closer. As if some rough edge had grazed him, in a swift focus he could see them that day. The girl very cool, and his brother with the smile, the flustered look, some crazy excitement that made his whole face slightly unfamiliar. Doug was the kind who always had worn a solid expression, since way back in high school. Or earlier. Even his biggest heats were under control. Doug never flapped in his life. . . .

Rion looked back at the lawyer, who wasn't asking a lot of questions or making lousy secret notes like the doctors. On a risky impulse, he decided to tell a little more than he'd meant to. Maybe it would add up to some answer?

2

· · · · · · · · · ·

I don't get it, these skull doctors ask me—did I ever
have some secret envy of Doug? I gave it to them
straight, I said, "You're damn right and it was no
secret."

When I was little I used to pray every night that
I'd have his brains and his grades and his looks. I
never was *jealous*, if that's what they mean. Because
Doug's always been decent, being four years older.
I know guys that have brothers two years older, but
Doug never was like that.

He even understands the other generation. Not that I don't, only I never know what to say that they'd care to listen to. Like the way he used to hustle my father about beautifying the riverfront—Pop's president of the Real Estate Board. By the time Doug would get through, Pop was nodding around like he suddenly got caught in the United Nations.

That type of thing always did grab Doug very hard. I guess it was his first year off at school, he did this term paper on Harlem—all about babies getting chewed on by rats and cockroaches in the coffee. And little kids on junk. He was so hung up, he didn't breathe twice the whole Christmas holidays. Damn, it bugs me when somebody gets excited.

Why couldn't I have come home that day and he'd be alone and glad to see me, and everything would've turned out different? Maybe—I don't know. Or if I'd played it cooler somehow? But right then, I didn't think too much about it—I was so beat.

All at once, I was dead. I flattened out on my bed right like that with my shoes on. I didn't even take a shower until later, when I came to.

Listen, I don't have to tell about that evening? All it did was foul things up—I acted like a collection of mixed idiots. Anybody in their right mind would have stayed upstairs forever, only I was about to starve. And I thought they'd gone out. It was so still in the house it woke me up. My ears were practically ringing, almost like there'd been a lot of yak going on somewhere a minute ago. But I thought they'd left, so help me, or I'd never have gone down there in nothing but my trunks.

After I took a quick shower, I didn't shave, I just dragged on some swim trunks and a beach robe, which is the way I always dress at home when it's hot. How should I know they're lurking out in the kitchen? You usually talk along, if there's a girl around. There she is, putting out this little food on the table—slivers of cheese and ham. I don't see how she cut them so thin, our knives aren't that sharp. And hard-boiled eggs that she scraped out the insides and mashed and put them back again. Doug's sitting there like he couldn't get his teeth loose from his pipe.

So I didn't know what to do, I was already at the door. I said sort of, "Well well, sorry to bug in here, I thought everybody went to a movie."

Shirli goes into a big hostess act, holds out her hand—and it was only the kitchen and I *lived* there. She says, "Ah, the young hunter, home from the hills—what can I fix you? How about some cool baloney, there's plenty of that around tonight." She gives Doug a look, so they'd been having some kind of fight. But all the time she goes on talking to me. "You look more like Swiss cheese on good brown rye—how about a hero sandwich? In honor of your escape—you did say you escaped from somewhere, didn't you? Not all of us are able to manage that." With this jewelry around her neck and the big bracelets, they did make her look like one of the slaves, sort of. In this white silk blouse real loose in front. She says, "Bid me, I'm yours to command."

Not that I let it bother me, I said, "Don't worry, I'll fix myself something hot." I had to eat something, I was stuck together inside. That thin stuff, I could've swallowed everything on the table just for openers. I felt like a steak at least. All I had to eat since noon the day before was one lousy frog leg.

That fascinated Shirli all to hell. She keeps watching me—I know it's no way, to throw a frozen steak right on in the pan, but I couldn't wait. And there was some corn on the cob, too. I guess I talked along, it makes me itch when everybody's shooting a whole lot of looks.

Anyhow Shirli did most of the talking. She'd make these cracks, not the way girls chat around—she halfway meant it. Like she tells Doug how I'm a genuine anachronism, means you should've lived a hundred years ago. I tried to remember it. A word like that could come in handy—some chick plays hard-to-get, you could flip it at her. "Baby, you're a livin', lovin' anachronism." I mean it's got class. Why Shirli called me that I don't know—unless it's because I was in my bare feet.

Doug mumbles something, about primitive types. "If you follow history back far enough," he says, "you'll end up in a cave."

"I wonder"—she's sore all right, the way people get when they smile like mad—"what would it feel like, to live in a cave? And *make* the history. You'd have to draw plenty of pictures on the wall—simple ones, so some bloodless scientist could explain you, centuries later in a postgrad course. 'Friday's lecture will be concerning the taste of raw meat.' " She kept looking at my steak. It got burned on the outside before it was hot through—I admit it looked pretty rugged. But Shirli was practically drooling, she wouldn't touch the thin stuff.

"Dear," Doug says, sort of around the edge of his pipe, "let's call a slight truce, hm? Rion wouldn't be interested in our differences of opinion on postgraduate school. Can't we, you know, observe the conventions and so forth?" He was hinting at her to shut up and make small talk, but it's going to take more than a hint.

"You're so right, pickle, dear," she says. "We

ought to be discussing current events. Tell me, oh-Rion, how did you happen to *need* a frog?"

I sure as hell wasn't going to get into that, so I kept it vague. I said, "I've been on the road. You get hungry."

"Basic. Very basic," she says, sort of leaning across at me so she can ignore Doug. "And what happened to the other frog leg?"

"Secret," I said. If I told her a ten-year-old kid gave me one and he ate the other, well I mean what business is it of hers, you know? Mostly she could hardly stand me digging into that steak. Before it gets too much for her, she finally tears away and goes over to the window—the way girls look out at the sky, sort of showing off a little.

"Old pickle"—she always called Doug that, some sort of pet name—"do you remember when we had secrets? So long ago—six months—when we were young? That night we sneaked away from the spring dance and sat out under the sky? We cooked up a whole lovely scheme—you were to get named to the Space Program, so you could secretly stall the whole rotten thing. By losing the files—that's how you were going to do it! Misplace hundreds of government files, so the sky would stay free and man couldn't create traffic jams out across the stars. That was a beautiful dream."

"That was a joke!" Doug snaps. It killed me, the way he sat there grinding his pipestem to a soft pulp. "At the tone, the time will be exactly right to grow up. At least that's how it looks from where I sit," he says.

But she just floats back in my direction. "Rion, do you think the sky's a joke? The Fates used to take it very seriously, who they elected to their heavens. Talk about history, those were the days. A woman could even aim for one of the gods if she was up to the game."

That's the kind of way some of these college girls talk. I've heard them before—I never could keep up with it. So all I said was, "When it comes to history, don't look at me. I almost flunked the stuff."

"That's better than getting hooked on grades," she says, still bouncing it off me to get back at Doug somehow. "It's a hard habit to kick—some people never do. They get permanently smothered by the big snow-job." Meaning college, I guess. She says, "Even if you can't invent fire, at least go out and commit something brave."

Damn her, it kind of needled me. I already just about sold myself how you *have* to go to some school—everybody does. So I didn't appreciate her making cracks about it. I kept wondering why Doug didn't move in—boy, if she'd been my date. I figure he's maybe lining up some choice remark where he could still be a gentleman, but it would put her down to the size of an ice cube. In the meantime, it's me she kept crowding. Sort of half hitched onto a chair right across the table, telling me what to go and do?

So I said, "Me, I'm not going anywhere but upstairs again. How'd you care to finish my steak? You sound like you could use it." I didn't mean anything, I just get that way when I'm pushed.

Well, Doug jumps up, you'd think a blowtorch bit him. "What sort of way is that to talk to my fiancée?" he yells at me. "Can't you kindly be at least a little civilized? You're old enough now to have a few manners—Mother's certainly *tried* to teach you the social graces." He was practically raving.

It kind of shook me. For him to chew me out? He never did it before, he doesn't have to get sore—he's won every argument we ever had. All I could figure was that crack about "fiancée"—it's the first I knew he was *serious* about her.

So what I did, I went on down to the garage to check on my car. I was going to throw a few clothes on and get clear out of there, to the YMCA or somewhere. But that's the kind of day it was—the heap won't start. I had an old clinker of a battery, you know, you don't buy new when you're heading off to camp all summer.

Anyhow, I thought nuts to that, I'm going to bed. In fact I said so when I went back past the kitchen —I said it real loud, so Doug would be sure I wouldn't be around for about sixteen hours. Only I don't think he heard me, he was watching Shirli polish off the rest of my steak.

Funny how you could live in your own room for years and never really notice it. Maybe I was just glad to get back up there, but it looked completely great. Especially since I was about to get gone. Pretty soon, I thought, I'll be picking my own shack.

I don't mean some dorm off at school, but when that was over with. After I'd put in a few rounds with some dictionaries, which you need if you don't want to look like you've got egg on your face around a babe like Shirli. Doug always did say, you have to get mature. Only I wished he wouldn't be mature over a weird sister like her.

I heard a lot of little yakkety-yak going on down in the kitchen, and I wouldn't want them to think I was listening. So I turned on the TV, I've got a portable, and I opened the window—you need it when you've been out in a lot of real air. Nothing out there but a whole lot of dark. I could imagine I was anywhere.

Wild. I thought about rooms—cheap ones, you'd have to settle for sometimes. But so you slap a few pinups on the wall, turn on the transistor, you're home. It's all I ever did around our own house. Oh, I knew I'd miss some things, like to wander down and drag out a steak if I felt like. But hamburger comes off the same cow. Mainly you're on your own —I began to feel it bearing in on me. Those crazy crickets or whatever they are out in the trees, the same as they've sounded every summer since I could remember. That's when I began to know it was really over.

Even my high school graduation picture looked old already. Lord knows why I stuck it up on the wall—with Scotch tape, it didn't add a whole lot to anything. I looked like some deadpan dummy back in the fourth row. When I thought about it, I had to admit I could've sweated harder this last year, if there'd ever been any point.

And all of a sudden, lying across my bed watching a bunch of fools cut up on this variety program on the TV, for some unknown reason I got the point. I started to see all those clowns as people—not just that they were making big money. But they were real, they were in gear, even if they were corny. They were so *busy*. And I wasn't. I started to feel like that a few times before, but I always got over it. You have to keep measuring everything by high school until you're out. There's no hurry, you're still ticketed for a dumb kid.

Now, I thought, I've got to buy the ticket myself. I better shape up. You should be able to picture yourself. It's odd—the only time I ever could do that was when I used to talk to a friend of mine. I've got this friend, but he won't be back for about five to ten years. So all the more, I wished I could bull around with Doug.

When I happened to turn off the TV—I couldn't take that music—I heard them going at it down there in the kitchen. Not loud, but they were arguing. I kept saying to myself, "You tell her, boy."

And then when I turned off the radio—the music was lousy—before I turned the TV on again, I heard them laughing. Doug's a—naturally—a happy kind of guy. Or he was.

. . . .

The lawyer rearranged his knees and tried to settle deeper into the hospital chair. Something he wanted to ask—Rion could feel it worrying him. "Did I say the wrong thing?"

"No, son, I'm not sitting in judgment. But I do

seem to be missing a few pieces of the picture. You say you'd just begun to think about college that day coming home. And yet your parents tell me they tried to discuss the subject all last year."

"The Institute, they kept trying to sell me on. This military-type prep school. Damn right, I wouldn't talk about it."

"But your high school—they usually blanket the subject like a brush fire, when you get to be a senior. Low grades or not. Didn't you have a guidance counselor?"

The idea of Mr. White helping you plan any type of important thing such as where you might maybe go to college gave Rion a muggy feeling that he thought he should, in all decency, try to hide. "Listen, don't blame him, sir. He had his hands full, trying to get me through Trig. No joke—he's O.K., we got along. Mr. White his name was, Mom's crazy about him. She says he's a fine-looking man, which he is, only not the way she says it—he's not more than about thirty-five. Lord, you don't figure she'll bring him in on this deal, do you? Get him to spilling a lot of stuff to these doctors, and I've had it."

"What harm could it do? If you were on good terms—"

"Oh sure. At least they're supposed to like everybody, but I think he really did like me. Only he knew I wasn't oriented. You know, I didn't know what I was doing there all this year. I shouldn't have let on, but he had this way of listening, like he was interested. You feel you ought to explain—he kept saying he knew I could get Trig if I tried. So I told him, if there was anything practical to it, like if there's five guys drawing cards and you got three hearts, what's the odds on getting two more? And figure it fast while the game's on the move. Only I shouldn't have mentioned it, he'd get this scaly look around the edges. But I couldn't tell him how it really was, how every time I'd try to settle down and study I'd get off onto thinking. I wouldn't even have gone back to high this year if it wasn't for Nick." Rion bit down on it fast, but the name came out—the way it happens when you get talking along, halfway confidential to somebody who keeps listening.

The lawyer screwed his eyebrow up, as if to say "Nick who?"

"This friend of mine," Rion admitted. If his parents even suspected he was ever buddy with a gambler and an older type at that . . . "Excuse me, I'd rather not talk about him. Anyhow, I did go back and graduate, with the diploma and every-thing, which was so great with everybody we didn't get into some new problem right then. Of course, what it was, the folks were going ahead anyhow behind my back. Maybe they did sort of hint around, I don't remember. Or else they figured I still wouldn't listen to them." He tried to think. "We were all in a hurry—everything got so complicated, with me trying to get off to the camp and them packing for their trip. They decided to wait until they got back—at least that's the way Doug spilled it. I mean, explained it. I mean—well, how if I just go on and tell it like it happened?"

3

· · · · · · · · · ·

I'll say this, Doug probably wouldn't have spilled
any beans if he wasn't all in stitches over this fe-
male.

I mean I can't imagine how you'd have to feel, to
consider getting married even slightly, so I'm not
blaming him or anything. For me, girls are to go
with pizza after the game. Any of them look like
they've got a lifetime guarantee, I shake off very
fast.

But Doug's different. He always did like to hang

around the house, cut the grass. I cut it too, but he enjoyed it. And he plays bridge. He can't see poker, he says there's no skill to it. If he'd ever once watched a guy like Nick . . .

But that's not the point. Where was I? Yeah, that next morning, Monday morning. If he was still in some mood I was ready to shove off, even though I did only half finish my breakfast when I heard him coming down.

But he seemed so normal again. Strolled on in, pajamas and all—snitched a piece of bacon off my plate. "Very unique. Will you give me your recipe?" Old joke, goes back to when I took cooking in junior high. I was going to be one of these hot chefs the hotels kidnap from each other on account of their secret recipe. Doug always kids me.

I can't do it—pretend nothing happened. So I said, "Listen, I'm sorry if I put my foot in it last night."

He brushed that off like nothing. "I don't know why I blew my stack. Not your fault, though— Shirli pointed it out in her own marvelous way, how you were just meeting her on her own ground. She hates hypocrisy worse than poison ivy, and so do I. Isn't she a dream?"

I tried to listen like, sure, great. He's all clinched up, telling how he met her at some sorority tea which was about to drag him under until she came around circulating this petition. Nothing really "proletarian"—I think he meant she wouldn't go so far as to walk in some picket line. Her family is very rigid, he says, but she personally is trying to get involved. How did it go—"She wants to feel involved in everything and everybody on this entire pitiful earth." And if it gets a little wild sometimes, he's trying to swing with it.

"Patient handling," he tells me in a private tone. "You have to know the delicate feminine id."

That id thing, I began to get the drift. Like ego and complexes and stuff, Mr. White could kill you with it.

"Id—that's everything, all you'll ever be and do," Doug is trying to explain to me. This year he got hooked on the subject from some teacher, Phillipson —the name kept flapping around like a flag. "It was pure fate that sent me to his class—I was beginning to doubt myself. Mr. Phillipson untangled all that. It's perfectly natural to have secret fears." I forget all of it. You try out your impulses and maybe discover you're a sex maniac, so you learn to control it. Not that Doug put it like that, but I got the idea. He's afraid he might overdo things with Shirli, he's so off his nut about her. "I'd better simmer down, it's a very heady thing," he says. How she stimulates him, only in a noble way—very pure—and he's bound he's going to analyze it.

I doubted if Shirli would buy too much of that, but I didn't say so. He sure was sold.

"To know thyself—" He goes on and on, about your inmost feelings. The type stuff you read in magazines: Take this test and see if you're neurotic. I always thought it was funny as hell, but he's a hundred percent serious.

So I said, "Is Shirli part of the bag?"

He grins around. "She's the whole of it, for me. Everything! She's keen and deep and warm, and terribly bright and also terribly sensitive." Because she's been turning him down all along when he proposed. Especially since now she found out he's going for the Ph.D.—she says he might be *too* much in love with her.

I asked, "Well, are you?" I was hinting around.

He laughs—talk about high, he was floating. "Love is a worn-out word. For an old generation, old people, old religions. The real thing is to be goaded! Shirli's mind is as brilliant as a diamond solitaire."

I agreed she's got a great little cutting edge. "Then all that, last night, was O.K.? I thought you looked a little chopped."

Very confidential he tells me, "The truth is, I was

undergoing a little self-discipline and it got away from me, there when I snapped at you. Sorry, tiger, none of it was your fault. We'd been having an argument when you came down. About college." He's decided to go back next fall and hit the books some more, and it didn't exactly rock Shirli.

Me either. I said, "You *got* a degree. Why more?"

"To stay ahead of the pack. Everybody these days has a bachelor's, so the M.A. is only a slight leg up, and the Ph.D. doesn't hurt a bit, not a bit. Shirli would see it, if she wasn't going through a period of disappointment about education."

I could hardly blame her for that. Here he's saying it's not near enough to scrape through four years —I mean, imagine *me* with a Ph.D.? But he's going on, how it's necessary to prepare yourself for the marketplace—emotionally and spiritually.

I said, "You mean all that just to go out and find some *job?*"

And right then something skidded slightly. I can't explain it, like you feel your wheels hit a soft spot.

Doug gets up. "I'm a dog, talking about myself when you've got troubles. I should be lending you the wisdom of my advanced years. What's the new misfortune, old buddy? What ended your career at Camp What's-it?"

I told him, "I got fired, that's all. Let's forget it."

"My boy"—he's sort of corning it up—"you are acquiring a job record which, to be kind about it, has a strong aroma."

So I tried to play it light too. "Yes, your honor, and did you know your fly's unbuttoned?"

"How did it happen this time?" he keeps on at me.

I wasn't going to tell him all that, he'd just start analyzing the whole thing like a problem. But I wanted him to know I really was fired. I signed a contract with the camp, I wouldn't want him to think I walked out on it.

"Come on," he says, "it must've been spectacular, judging by the way you looked yesterday, towering there on the edge of the carpet." He kept walking up and down, so finally I told him.

"I got lost. I got good and damn lost, they had to send a chopper to find me. I should've stayed down in the woods, too—it was great, being nowhere."

He didn't exactly believe it. "You know, this could all haunt you in later years. You go looking for some work you really want, and they'll say, 'Who's this, old Rion Fletcher? Can't hire him, look how he loused up all those summer jobs.' "

"You don't get the picture," I told him. "I'm keeping in condition so when I get canned from bigger things, I'll know how to land on my feet."

"Seriously—" he says.

"So who's kidding? It's like a knack—some guy that's never been fired in his life, the first time he gets the thumb he's going to flip. My advice to you is to get in practice before you're too old." And all at once, I wished I kept my mouth shut. Something —the way his thongs kept squeaking on the floor . . . I said, "Summer jobs are a lot of lather anyhow. You had the right idea, to improve your skull all these years. I been thinking I ought to look into it—like what kind of fool school will maybe take in a guy with a low score like me?"

"No problem about that"—but his mind isn't on it—"some good little Tech maybe. Time to think about it after you've had a couple of years at the Institute."

"No Institute, I'd look rotten in a uniform," I said. I didn't even think about it until he lets out this yip.

"What? After the folks sprained a collar button to get the thing lined up?"

"Lined up *how!*" I was thinking, how come Pop never heard me all those times I told him no thanks? And then it really hits me. "How *could* they do that if we didn't even know I was going to graduate?"

"Now don't jump to any conclusions." Doug began to talk like somebody pulled a string. "They knew you were in some sort of a bind all this year, they only wanted to help—" On and on.

I said, "How many people did Mom twist the arms of, to clinch it that I'd squeak through?" She's the kind—not just a few teachers, probably the whole school board. She wouldn't mind if she went to the Mayor.

"If you will kindly simmer down—" Doug really did look worried by then. "Listen, Rion, forget I told you. They wanted to do it their own way when they got back from the cruise—it all came to a head just when they were leaving."

"So they lost my address and got writer's cramp and didn't have a dime for the telephone. Well, you know what?" I yelled. "They can take the Institute and stick it up a cold chimney and forget about me and college of any type."

"Nonsense, don't be childish," he says. "Of course you're going on to some school."

If there was anything could've lit two more matches under me. "And be some phony. Pretend I'm a wise guy, maybe someday have a piece of paper to hang on the wall and impress people? Well, I'll tell you what I'm going to do—I'm going out and get a job. Something it takes a little guts for, which you don't learn in class, waiting for the grades to get posted. I guess I know how many marbles I got.

And if anybody asks me where I went to school, I'll tell 'em—right out on the hot sidewalk, buster, where you learn to make your own music."

I still . . . it still gets me sore.

. . . .

Outside the hospital window, the afternoon sky had taken on a vivid yellow glare. Rion stared at it irritably, the fierce haze crisscrossed by the black mesh of the screen. Heavy wire screen, like on the windows of the gym, except this would be one hell of a place to play basketball . . . And then he knew what it was there for.

Looking away from the brightness, he could hardly see for a minute—the whole room seemed shadowy.

The lawyer moved quietly; for a big man with a lot of rumpled summer suit on, he hung loose. At least, somewhere along about then he went away. But he left a feeling that he'd be back.

4

· · · · · · · · · ·

Yes sir, I guess I feel better this morning. Food's
real great—tastes like they wash the dishes in
Drano. But I can't kick. It'll be worse, probably,
wherever I'm going.

Those doctors were here again. They keep having
this idea I've got an inferiority jag. No matter what
I say—I guess if I ever do decide to knock myself
off, I'll have to blow my brains out, to show people
I've got a few.

School, they make too much over. Sometimes it

happens to be convenient to play it stupid—you build yourself up that way, so when you do something dumb you won't feel quite so lousy embarrassed. These smart types, if they ever fall on their faces it hurts worse, you know? At least I always felt more comfortable not being too much.

Only I never thought my folks noticed—I mean, maybe they thought all along I'm really short-headed. All that foul-up with Trig, that was sort of a game I played with Mr. White to see if he could ever think of one good reason I should beat my brain against it. But you take the I.Q. tests—they all said I had some. And in my junior year, I still was hanging in there on grades.

English, I was even fairly good. Of course if I talked the way you're supposed to, I'd feel like a freak, but I know how. I memorize O.K., long enough for some test. Or I used to, up till this year. I don't know, lately I couldn't sit still. Like if I didn't get in my heap and get some breeze moving, cruise around. Or walk up onto the north side.

I never drive up there. Park on the street, too many things happen to a car with a Cedar Woods sticker, even an old crate like mine. That's what I like about the north side, it's different. Something's going on in those sausage markets and the Chinese laundries and pinball joints. Even the little kids all look like they're carrying some kind of news buttoned under their shirts. They got no worries about the territory we took in the Mexican War, they got their own turf to fight for. It's here and now, you know? They wouldn't even care if the Commies took over the whole downtown business district, because nobody's going to take over the north side—nobody.

Downtown is a pain anyhow—I never should have gone there that day, all splintered up like I was. I didn't want to, but the buses go right on down the same old groove to City Hall. And I had to take a bus. I left the order at our filling station to come charge my battery, but I didn't feel like waiting. Even the bus fumbling along was better.

I kept trying to sell myself a lot of things—how it was going to be great, not to waste four years at college. You can pack some real experience under your belt in four years, some kind of trade, maybe you could go into business for yourself. I had this idea I wasn't ever going to make a great employee type, not the luck I had with jobs. Doug was right, I've got a crummy record. And I don't see how I could've helped it, either.

That deal at Ginnis and Clark, I walked out at ten-thirty in the morning, that's *worse* than getting fired. Yeah, last summer it was. Imagine me working for a deep-dish corporation like that? The lifeblood of the mail room. No, there's nothing to tell—I wouldn't have got into it at all except that when Doug came home for vacation, I wished I could understand even half of what he kept talking about.

He was taking some extension course in banking or finance or something. The way he'd scowl around at Pop—"It's one bear of a market we've got right now! Holding my breath, boy!"

And Pop would shake his head. "Yep, new housing starts are way off. It's the tight money."

Old Doug'd swivel his pipe, left to right. "If you ask me, tight money is our last chance. Do you know what our balance of payments is *right this damn minute?*" And he'd be off, saving the country. Lord, it kills me when somebody's all worked up.

And Pop was so glad I was interested, I couldn't hurt his feelings after he went and lined up this mail-room job. At first it seemed O.K., too—some guy shove a telegram in your hand and say "Rush that over to Export." I'd probably have stuck there all summer if I didn't start eating lunch with Meisner. Ran the photostat—you wouldn't think anybody who does that would have some great ambition to raise mink? He'd damn near cry when he talked about it—only had twelve years yet to go before the company retired him. And that's when it began to get me.

I'd see some girl sharpening her pencils—sixty-five. And the men were worse, these kind that sit at their desks? Even the boss, reading his *Wall Street Journal*—sixty-five. He didn't have long to go, he was half dead.

So when the personnel manager asks me, "How about signing up for next summer, you can start qualifying for our pension plan," I know he was trying to do me a favor, but all of a sudden I thought: in exactly forty-seven and a half years. And that was that. But I'm sorry I didn't give them two weeks' notice, like Doug and Pop and everybody on earth gave me a lecture on.

Being downtown brought it back, very loud and lousy. I knew I'd better not foul up many more times. So I kept trying to think what I *wanted* to do. I know, Mr. White always acted like you should be born wanting something, but that's because he never looked into it. Always telling about the advantages of this and that—the more people talk about success, I keep thinking there must be something better.

Downtown is no place to figure it, either. All those store windows, full of stuff—what's so wonderful you've got to have it or bust? Wishing for a lot of junk you'll just have to buy all over again next year. Or whenever the neighbors get a new model. I mean, Mom's like a blue streak around our house, new appliances—how you could get all grooved up about an electric can opener.

Me, all I need is enough cash for a six-pack or a ball game once in a while. But a whole pile? I guess it's pretty thick of me not to get it. If I could work up a good sweat over money, all the rest would be easier to figure. Because if you don't want that, then what?

So I tried looking at a surfing rig in the sport goods—just take off for Hawaii maybe. But that didn't work, either. Because to be a successful beach bum, you've got to not care about going anywhere. And for some reason that made me feel kind of sick.

Or maybe it was all those DON'T WALK signs—it's like you're on a string and somebody has hold of the other end. That's why I kept drifting on down to the riverfront, which is where I wound up. At least along the docks you see some action. Those tugs shoving the big stupid barges, it even looked O.K. for a minute. Cast off the ropes, slue around and head on out of there—scramble the water up. You own your own boat, nobody can tell you when to blink. But I didn't hang around too long down there. Talk about pollution—if they'd call it what it really is, maybe people would do something about it.

Everything kept stringing me up that day, I couldn't relax.

"Relax, relax," Irv kept saying. Irv Moore, that's

this character I know—I was never real buddy with him, but you get tired of messing around alone. Only I guess I was bothering his game—we were shooting pool. I kept fidgeting around and, like I said, up on the north side don't do it.

"What's the difference?" Irv says. "If you turn out to be a slob, it's all your folks' fault—ask anybody. The more your parents keep leaning on you, it's very unhealthy. I saw a whole TV program on how old people keep lousing up their kids. So *relax!*" He's got some sense of humor, I should've slugged him. I think I could take him, all right.

Well, naturally I was sore, him making cracks about my parents. Maybe I get a little irritated at them, but they mean O.K. They're only trying to be like everybody else—it's not their fault. They never ruined my life or anything.

I told him, "I don't figure on *being* a slob, you can have the complete monopoly."

"Grow up," he says. "With antipoverty, it's practically patriotic to not work—you want to put all those government types out of a career? Then your old man couldn't cry about his taxes he pays. Everybody needs to cry, especially about how their kids have gone to the dogs. Don't crumb up their simple pleasures."

I could've handled him—his face is no color at all—I could've laid him out cold. But you don't make that kind of scene around the doghouse. If Nick had been there, he'd have done it with a few kind words—he could slice Irv up like a pickle and never miss a shot.

So I tried, I said, "For your information, I had a real great childhood. There's never any fight going on around our house like at some people's homes I know." I mean, what's to argue about? Mom's not going to tell Pop how to sell real estate and he's got no complaint about how many meetings she goes to, she's very civic-minded. It probably makes him a lot of good will.

Irv says, "I wouldn't even want folks that didn't paste each other once in a while. Saturday nights at our place is better than the wrestling matches. How do you know where your old man stands if he never blows his wig?"

I shouldn't admit it, but I thought about that. Especially lately, with them trying to get rid of me off to this sanitarium. I really don't know where they stand, about anything. Oh, I know they love me and all, that's not what I mean.

· · · · · · · · · ·

Rion stopped short when he heard himself say it aloud—the thing that had been kicking around his brain these nights. He hadn't meant to get into that, and yet here was this lawyer—a gold-plated legal eagle, who ought to know a few answers. Even if he did look like just some middle-aged joe with his knees crossed and thumbs hooked into his belt, the face had been through some wars.

"All this about freedom"—Rion knew it came out smart, but it was the truth—"if you ask me, they're scared of it. Like why should they act as if it's some crime to stroll up onto the north side, I mean a guy my age?"

"Who acts like—?"

"My folks. When they found out I even *went* there."

"Maybe they just wish you could be spared some of the two-bit cynicism of a punk like Irv."

"O.K., he's a punk. If you don't ever meet a few, how do you know the difference? Sure, the view's dirtier down on street level, but at least when you're finding out stuff, you don't go soft. In fact, there's some real great people over on the north side if they were really created equal, the way it's supposed to be. That's another thing—can I ask you? Take my folks, they play bridge for money at the Country Club, no sweat. So why's that different from the guys shoving the pot up, in the back room at the doghouse? Just because they don't have a golf course out in the alley behind? Listen, if there's a law says you can't gamble, but there's another one says you have to pay income tax on what you win, and you can't even deduct your losses, which would it be better to go to jail to the tune of? If you don't live in Cedar Woods, I mean?"

The attorney didn't do the kind of take most people would; he didn't argue. He didn't even pretend he had a good answer. In a sort of grunt of concession he said, "So—you've begun to notice the inconsistencies on the part of the management? Join the club, son. It's what makes some of us study law."

"Yeah, Nick said there'd always be lawyers. And cops and undertakers. But if a person's not smart enough to be a mouthpiece—"

"There are other ways to square the differences."

Rion felt a strong impulse to bust him loose from that cool. "Square, like what? Play along, get with it? Like these people, my pop's friends—the insurance guys, investment-and-loan and all? You want to know the real reason I got loused up this year, I started listening to people. Not just hearing, you always hear stuff, but when you begin to think what they said. It stacks up to, you stand around and get fat and the whole rest of your life is one colossal bore, because you *don't* sweat over the differences. If you do, so be an oddball and drop dead. Talk about square—you mean sell out."

"I mean you don't fight City Hall with your bare

fists. You study the scene and wait till next election."

All at once there was something so familiar about that twist of words, the flicker of keenness in the lawyer's eyes, as if he were looking forward to the game—a memory jumped up that almost throttled Rion. For a minute, the guy had sounded exactly like Nick.

He dug his elbows back into the pillows and tried to forget it. "Where were we, anyhow? That day with Irv—he says some guys were going to get together out at The Diner, like nine o'clock, which sounded better than nothing. So I started out there about eight-thirty and that's when I got in my first flap with the cops."

"Hold it, you had to go home and get your car. Doug was there? Shirli?"

"Yeah, yeah, but all you need is the part about the State Trooper."

"I need the parts you don't want to tell."

"But it makes me sick. Listen, sir, could we knock this off?"

5

· · · · · · · · · ·

I was afraid you wouldn't be back—me, funking out that way yesterday. Most people would say, "Well, there's another crummy kid, shot to hell and good riddance." You're kind of different from what I always pictured lawyers. Anyhow, thanks for coming.

This is one deep mess of molasses I'm in, I know it. I didn't sleep all night, thinking about everything. First I thought, what am I *doing*, telling all this? And then if I go back over it, I swear I don't think I'm soft in the brain. And that's what I need to convince everybody, so I'll try to tell it all—even if some of it wasn't too sweet.

Like when I got home that evening. I walked up the next block and cut across yards to come in the back way, just in case. And I was right. In the refrigerator, fresh groceries—I always look when I go past, it's a habit. Steaks and about ten ears of sweet corn, so Shirli was around. Across the chair there's a skirt, the kind girls keep handy to button over their shorts. Also Doug's thongs under the kitchen table.

I thought, let's stick right out here. I grabbed a sandwich, there's always plenty of liverwurst and cheese on hand, and I threw some other junk on. I wasn't real hungry, but I didn't have any lunch, so I drank this quart of milk while I'm deciding. Just to get in the heap and drive off, it'll look too obvious. But if I go in the front of the house . . .

So I kept trying to make plenty of noise, I dropped a few things and shoved the chairs around. And pretty soon I heard some form of life. If it was Doug, I didn't know what to say, after the way I churned around this morning. I hate anybody who's all the time apologizing.

When he came in, he looked odd—or at least he didn't look like you ought to if you're trying to knock around in just a pair of pants. They were really great slacks—brand-new Dacron. But you ought to wear a shirt with them. Or maybe it was the belt, tooled leather with a silver monogram buckle. He never wore anything *like* that before.

He knew it too. Kept glancing down at his ribs. "Shirli and I were just sitting around, keeping cool. Come on in and join us, buddy." Man, was he nervous. Partly at me, I guess. "When you went out of here this morning, you were talking fairly wild," he says. "I've been worried about you."

"Don't give it a thought," I told him. "You got your own head to scratch, and I'll try to keep out of the way. You explain to her how I had to go meet some friends and I'll probably bunk down with one of them, so don't look for me to come home tonight."

"Hold it." He gets between me and the door. "We were counting on you for dinner. Shirli, too— she wants to help. We both want to see you through this crisis." He's being so kind, it just about kills me. He says, "I mean it, you won't be interfering with anything. You're part of our family—in fact, if you'll stick around, you can add to the image I'm trying to build."

I hated to tell him, but I didn't hardly feel like being part of his image. I didn't want to ask what it was, even.

"You see"—he gets hush-hush—"Shirli has lived

in a pretty false society atmosphere, she's naturally leery. Of practically everything conventional. She has this impulse to be part of the earth. I've got to convince her that she can do it and still be a lovely young suburban matron."

I could've told him, *never* call a chick anything like that.

He says, "I'm trying to make her feel at home here, and you can help. She relates to you, for some reason. And you seemed to get what she was driving at last night, maybe a bit better than I did." He hated to have to say it.

I thought, I better clear out right now. "Sorry," I told him, "but this kind of deal is not my dish—good luck, though." And I eased on out of there. All I hoped was my battery was back up to full.

It was, only the ammeter was kicking. I knew I needed new brushes, and I got this weird idea— suppose I might want to take off fast, for anywhere. Without a whole lot of goodbys. It came and went, but it was the best idea I had all day. So I figure, my tools are handy, I can shove in some new brushes in ten minutes. How should I know? I'm hardly into the generator and there she is, Shirli.

If there's one thing I can't stand it's a woman around a car. So I try to hint she ought to chase herself back in the house. Even if we do have a pretty high fence along the side where the driveway is—which is where I was working. The neighbors are the kind who've got thin eyes from looking out the venetian blinds. They'd practically faint if they ever saw some girl out in our drive in that getup.

I guess you'd call it a playsuit, only it didn't have enough buttons down the front. It made her look like a handful of nothing. And the more I shook her off, she kept putting out these stupid remarks about the heap. I always like a lot of chrome under the hood, the manifolds and gas lines and like that. She kept talking about its beautiful "character" or something. She says, "No wonder there are no women in your life"—though how should she know?—"they couldn't compete with this wild playmate of yours." And it's only a '57 Chevy, the chassis is.

All the time I'm making a few remarks like I hoped she wouldn't catch cold, and excuse me, I was busy, and watch out, you'll get grease on you. I was hinting, for cornsake! But she goes on about how it must be great to speed through the night with the motor throbbing, or some fool thing.

I said, "Listen, Doug is probably biting his fingernails. Why don't you go throb a little at him, huh?" I didn't know how to say it any plainer.

"Doug is getting dressed. *He's* the kind who catches cold." And she screws her face up in one of those laughs—Doug called it "pixie" once, I'll buy that. She says, "Oh, his car is a sensible model—I knew that all along, of course. But he said it got wished onto him. He told me he'd really prefer a convertible. Do you think he meant it?"

"Yeah, sure," I told her. "He always did want a Mustang." And it's true. He took over the Dodge because Pop has to keep getting new cars in his business, and one year he gave his old one to Doug so he'd have something at least to get around in. Only it's real-estate blue. Pop has to have a color that doesn't make anybody mad; when you're in his business people hate you if they think you're getting rich off some deal. I tried to explain it to her—mostly I was trying to get the generator slung back in there.

With her walking around my elbows. She says, "I notice you didn't inherit any conservative tendencies." And she sort of runs her hand over the engine block, I could've slugged her.

Taking cracks at Doug—maybe he is kind of old-fashioned. Mom always told us to respect girls, which you do, if they really want it that way. Only you can bet most of them don't, including Shirli. Not that I cared, only I wished she'd shut up about my own brother's tendencies.

"He's one great guy, and you better believe it," I told her.

"He was—we had such fun off at school. Even if he's always been on the shy side, I thought I could change that. Only now"—she keeps looking up at the house—"since we came here, it's just the opposite. He's trying to domesticate me. Don't you think that's sort of a pity?" And she comes up all of a sudden, she's right under my arm, her hand kind of tickling the middle of my back.

I said, "You can cut that stuff right out," and I tightened down the bolts quick. I piled in the front seat and switched on the ignition. I didn't notice her moving in until she reaches through the front window—she has this gob of grease on her finger— and damn if she didn't plant it right on my mouth.

"A kiss," she says, "from your little eight-cylinder lover." And she kicks the front tire on her way back into the house. With that long hair.

So you can see why I wasn't exactly dying to tell about it. Also why I looked pretty ratty—I wouldn't have gone back in there to change clothes if I was on my way to meet St. Peter. Boy, I kept thinking, it's my own brother that's mixed up with her. How do you tell a guy that this girl he's engaged to has been making a play?

So maybe I did have my foot pretty deep in it when I got out to the county. At least the cop clocked me at seventy-two miles an hour. I wouldn't argue. If I did jaw around, it was when he said I must've been drinking, which was a lie. I was *not* out of focus, like he said. My coordination was perfectly O.K., I'm a damn good driver. I never got a ticket in my life, before then.

Anyhow after Blue Boy finished having his kicks, I did go slower. They radio every other state patrol in a hundred miles to watch out for you. I could feel 'em parked out there in the dark somewhere, keeping the old eye peeled for a crummy kid in a beat-up Chevy. So, like I said, I cooled off and tried to think. Only what I thought was, I did enough thinking for one day.

All I wanted was to make it to The Diner. Even if their jukebox was lousy lately, it didn't matter. We always make enough noise so it cuts the music. And that's what I felt like, plenty of action, even Irv with his saxophone imitation. Some pinballs going and the manager yelling at the waitress.

Only when I got there, the place was dead. The girl said she thought Irv and the guys went over to Crossroads, it was after ten by then. One thing I was sure—I wasn't going home that night. When the guys weren't at The Shack, which was where the fellow at Crossroads thought they went, I started back for The Diner. And then I thought, to hell with it.

I just headed the car off down a county road I

know, to an old gravel dump. There was nobody around, so I pulled in behind a pile of gravel. I never mind sleeping in my heap—I've done it plenty of times. Even at home you get tired of being upstairs, for some reason. I used to go down and goof off in the garage. I've got it figured out how to lie in the back seat—I was comfortable. I just let go. I thought, thank the Lord *that* damn day's over.

. . . .

Rion knew it had been more than that, but it's hard to tell somebody exactly what you were *really* thinking. Away out there in the nowhere feeling of the country. All that's left behind is some little poops of light over on the horizon. A reddish glow where the highways cross and everybody stops to talk it up in some roadhouse. Pretty puny against all that dark sky. Especially when the big heat lightning flared, way off west. He tried to remember what it was that had come over him. Just a few inches of something, like old age. . . .

6

. . . .

Odd, what it does to you—sleeping out. First down at camp that night we all got lost. And then in my car at the gravel pit, I get this feeling: now I'm on center. The rest of the show is wheeling around out there, I can lie back and choose where I get on board. Not that I had anything figured, but I felt like it was out there to *be* figured if I worked on it.

There were even some frogs. And the moon kept going in one direction, so I knew that was west. Which I'd have known anyhow if I wanted to think which way was town and where's the river from here. But I didn't. I'd rather pretend I didn't know anything except what I could make up my own mind about. Like west.

That's another difference between when I was a junior and this year, when I was flunking—exactly that, what I was just getting at. Every time somebody told me something, I kept thinking, "Who says?" Even when they were right. I can't explain it.

So now I had the whole thing in my lap and that was O.K. Completely O.K. and no regrets. My folks weren't around to settle stuff. I could think about them, in fact I liked them. I liked the hell out of them, way off in the Bahamas, having a great time. My mother's practically beautiful when she's playing bridge. Or golf, and all that. Pop—you can't tell. The only time I get an idea he's living it up is when some deal is cooking. You know he's onto something big by how much he belches.

That's what I needed right then. The only time I ever got that way was when I used to pitch for the Little League. For a while I even was going to end up in the majors—I had a damn sweet change of pace. But so do a lot of other guys, I don't kid myself.

And there's one *big* difference—when you're a little younger, you think you can do anything. This last year I couldn't kid myself a bit. Like I knew I couldn't take off at 2 A.M. for California with only a couple of bucks on me. You'd get busted for vagrancy an hour after you hit town.

Even if I drew out my whole bank account. The folks always give us a good allowance, but I used to blow most of mine on the car. And it takes at least a slight stake to go anywhere—some strange town you have to crawl around with a map. There's nobody to call up in a pinch. Which would be a good feeling—it's exactly what I wanted, but I wanted to do it right. So I figured I'd better stick here until I could roll up a little cash.

I thought, cornsake, there must be *something* I didn't mind too much in school. Like shop. We had this funny old guy, Mr. Giordello—a real sourball. Man, he made us hop, you'd think he was paying five bucks an hour for this stuff. Bookcases and magazine racks, I made Mom a sewing cabinet. She doesn't sew, she's got no time. The reason I took it on was all those drawers. Mr. Giordello was murder on drawers that don't hang up.

So you kick an idea around. I thought—all these new houses, why not? Apprentice first, build a couple of million forms for the cement, but sooner or later you get to hang doors, you work your way inside. And it's always a new job, a new house—right from scratch, new lumber. Someday hire a little crew of your own and you're in business. Crazy. I mean, to get all worked up over it—I bet I stayed awake most of the night, planning how I'd build a house. No windows unless there's a view. Just a bunch of wild skylights, those stars get under your skin. Well, maybe one window—to see the sun rise. Birds all tuning it up, those little bobwhites—they kill me.

As soon as it was light, I headed for home, but I was trying to take it easy. I sure as hell didn't want any more tickets. If they took away my license, I'd rather they'd cut off my feet. The last block to the house, I coasted all the way—my motor makes a pretty gutty sound and I didn't want to wake Doug. I did have to gun it a little to get into the garage. That's the one law Pop laid down: Don't leave it out where it'll mess up the scenery. So I slid in, I'm thinking, "Stay in bed, old buddy."

Somehow I didn't want to see him—not that I was sore or anything. But ever since I came home, I had to feel my way, stepping on cracker crumbs. Nothing had turned out easy, like I'd thought. And right then I didn't want to get in a new sweat over it. I wanted to keep accelerating.

But I'm hardly in my room before he waltzes in, keyed up like ten banjos. Gives me this big grin—I thought, *now* what went wrong?

"Hi, boy," he says. "Hope you didn't spend too

rough a night on somebody's couch. We didn't need all that privacy, actually. We're a little too old to dally around like a couple of kids."

Which means he didn't make out and that's what went wrong. I said, "You all have another blowup?"

"Just a little discussion. Were your ears burning?" He almost winked at me, I swear. "We were talking about you—we both feel you need our help, though we took—well, slightly different approaches. Big problem, old buddy, how to develop your potential. It's no snap."

And all along that's what I'd wanted to talk to him about. So don't ask me why I couldn't. Maybe because he called it "potential"—if there's any word that's a drag. Anyhow, what I did was start to take my clothes off. That usually does it, he gets out. I said, "I'm on my way right now to take care of that, about my potential."

But he goes to stand at the window with his back turned. "The Institute—"

"Is out," I told him and went on in to take a shower.

"I was only going to agree"—right behind my heels. "It's not your style at all, old buddy. On the other hand, if you don't have some kind of degree, you'd better buy a shovel."

"They got machines now to dig ditches," I said,

and I turned the jet on hard. But he kept on slanting around, yelling over the shower curtain.

"I think I could sell you on some very desirable aspects of campus life. There's more to it than meets the eye. It's nothing like high school, absolutely not the same animal."

"Maybe you got something there, but don't let it bug you," I said. "I'm in great shape. Maybe I don't ever make as big a bankroll as you do, which is O.K.—you sure have it coming. Me, I'll be happy slinging rivets or running a dozer or something." I didn't want to let him in yet on the carpenter angle until I had it nailed down. All I said was, "I got a couple of leads I'm working on right now."

"Well, good," only he didn't sound like it was good. "But I wish you'd let me *in* on this thing before you make any rash decisions. It might be the ruin of your subconscious—you can spend a whole lifetime fighting yourself. As Mr. Phillipson says, 'If you don't know exactly where you're going, *don't go*.' It's safer to wait."

"Only I am sure. I got to get downtown by nine." I was lying a little, pulling on some clean clothes. I tried to tie this tie I didn't have on since graduation.

"Will you *listen* to me," he says. "I know you're very emotional about all this, but you've got to admit—you do need help to get oriented."

Oriented. My own brother. I told him, "I'm sorry I got so lousy emotional at you yesterday, but I'm not now. I am perfectly damn calm—all I want to do is go get a job. An honest-to-john job, no more temporary, no more fooling around, no more school, *no sweat!*"

"Well, good luck!" he yells back at me. "You're going to need it, if you think it's so great to go through life with a shaggy brain."

I finally put the damn tie in my pocket. In a minute, I was going to need another shower.

He was sorry, too. He starts kind of punching me the way he used to. "All I wanted is to make sure you'll be home for supper. There are some aspects of all this I'd like to discuss with you. This is a turning point in your life. And if I can't exactly wave a wand, at least maybe I can just *slightly* show you a few angles."

When he acts straight with me I soften up like a sponge.

"Do you need money?" he says. "If you're short of cash—" Doggone, he can be nice. He says, "Dinner at six, huh?"

Lord, dinner. I said, "You mean with Shirli, too?"

For some reason he didn't exactly look at me, he sort of laughed like ha-ha. "She's going to cook it. Or fix it—I don't think she knows much about cooking. But bear with it, this is doing her good. I think she's beginning to sense the beautiful atmosphere Mother has created for us here in this household. At least Shirli feels very motherly toward you."

I didn't say a thing, believe me.

"Just a nice little family evening," he pleads around. So—well, I thought maybe he *needed* me. If I could help him—anyhow, that's how I finally said O.K. Some cockeyed idea that by the time I got home, I'd have my own scene under control and we'd all be flying our own flag—maybe the evening wouldn't be too bad. How you could keep on hoping stuff like that.

Of course it might have worked out all right, if I'd had any luck that day. Because I felt good, still. All the way downtown, the houses looked completely great. Even the crummy ones with the green gravel roofs. And the hokey lamps in the windows, I thought, we'll see about that.

I should mention I took the bus again. Those parking lots want your arm and a couple of teeth, and right then I was starting to save my money. Sounds weird now. Anyhow, I took the bus clear on into the station and looked up a mirror, didn't have any more trouble with the tie. I even got hungry.

They have a counter in the station and a girl

dishing the short orders. Not that she has anything to do with this, except she would have to be fat. They get that way when they pass out those coffee rolls all day. She must've weighed two hundred, and she looked like one hell of a nice girl—these very clear eyes that come out to meet you.

Besides which, she was good. She gave me five, six extra dabs of butter for the stack of wheats. Her hands were practically beautiful. I got this idea— you always think *something* when a girl hands you some home-style hashbrowns which she made her-self—I thought, a guy could do worse. It just came and went, but right away I could hardly eat. It's—I don't like to admit it, it's not fair or anything—but I got a whole flash of me tied up with some hippy girl that's got a lot of chins. And you've always thought if you ever did have a wife she'd be a com-plete doll—anybody does.

So all the time I was eating, she kept bringing me the whole pitcher of half-and-half for my coffee. Not on the make or anything, but she was handy. I really hated myself, no joke. I thought, there's one million women in the world that are a bunch of lying little fools and *this* kid has to have nice eyes. That's probably going to be the story of my life. All I could do for her was leave a decent tip.

She smiles like, thank you, call again. *Very* nice.

Well, it's nothing. Except you should never think of getting married, even temporarily. I just tried to concentrate on where I hoped they'd send me out first on a job—you know, the union. You got to be in a union to get a job with any building contractor in the state. Sure, there isn't a hiring boss will touch you. They contact the union and the union has a list in the office, guys who are available.

Pop always said it was a racket, to eliminate free-lancers and keep the wage scale higher than it ought to be. But I figured it was maybe a good thing to have a big outfit like them to go to bat for you when you need a raise. Those guys at Ginnis and Clark, they knee-walk fifty weeks out of the year so maybe they'd get a raise. Every time they grinned at the boss, you could read it all over them —"Five bucks, just a lousy little five bucks, you won't ever miss it."

Take carpenters, they are not kissing the toe of some contractor. They tell him, "I don't touch a shovel, buster, I'm a carpenter and if you want to make something out of it, I'll ask the field represent-ative to step around and explain it to you." They can pull every man off a job like that, some con-tractor start grinding them down. I was glad to be going to join, I was looking forward to it.

Huh. Should've known better, if I'd ever discussed

it with Pop. But he always had this idea I'd be an engineer, so we never talked about much else. Anyhow, the girl at the union office clued me in real fast. She practically laughs in my face. "Where you been since school let out, sonny boy? There's about two hundred fellows ahead of you on the waiting list." For apprentices. I didn't know you had to plead with somebody to get to be a lousy apprentice —they always get the short end of the stick, they do the dirty work. I thought the union would be happy to get anybody who'd *want* to apprentice.

After I filled the card out— She flips me this card. I don't know, some women it doesn't do them any good to be at a window with a cashbox and a switchboard, she was very important stuff around there. After I filled it out, she gives it a glance and does a slight double take. "You aren't any relation to A. R. Fletcher, I suppose?"

So—I don't know why, because Pop wouldn't mind me using his name—but anyhow I said, "No." Real quick.

And that was that, she puts the card in a file box, way at the back. "Call us every week or your name will be dropped. And don't let it stop you from finding some other type work, we're still on last year's list."

I don't know—when I got outside I just pulled

the tie off and crammed it in my pocket. I knew I'd played it stupid. Hell, I wanted the job. I thought, I ought to walk back in there and tell 'em, you're damn right I'm A. R. Fletcher's son. I kept saying it over, but I couldn't make it stick—the whole idea made me sick. I couldn't explain it, but to think how Pop—first the deal at high, and getting me those summer jobs, and entered in the Institute, and now he's not even in the country, but somehow he's still running the show. It was like I was surrounded.

Maybe that doesn't make sense. It sure doesn't to Pop. He found out about it since they got back, some subcontractor saw my name on the list. That's one more reason they figure I belong in the—you know—funny farm.

. . . .

Rion's voice tailed off into a sickly-sounding laugh. Because he still hadn't figured—*why*, for petesake, why couldn't he get with it? Everybody on earth knows it's how to operate to get anywhere. Use any name, any contact, keep lists of them—everybody you ever said "hello" to, you mention if it'll put you one-up. That's how the world kicks. If there was one thing, he thought, he should've learned listening to

Pop all these years. So why should it still stick in his craw?

Disgusted with himself, he glanced at the lawyer, and again the glint of expression reminded him of Nick. You'd swear this guy was interested. Except who's ever really bugged by some kid's opinion?

"Just thinking," the attorney said, as if in answer. "About what they mean when they spout about initiative. Make good, and so forth." His shoulders hunched, deep in the wrinkles of his coat. "Success stories make good reading, but if you don't write your own book—"

"Yeah." Rion grabbed it. "If you don't get there using your own blood, so join the weak!" And the scorn helped shore him up inside. "Only— Well, did you ever have to go hunting a job, right out of nowhere?"

7

· · · · · · · · · ·

I know I didn't go at it right. I just walked in and
said, "I'm looking for a job." They'd stare at me like
I just grew feathers on my ears. I guess you're supposed to write a letter, warn 'em you're coming.
Every place I went that day they'd say, "We didn't
advertise for any help." Which I never claimed they
did.

It just seemed reasonable that a lumberyard could
maybe use one more guy with shoulders. Or a couple of garages I went to—they had cars stacked up

waiting. But all they asked was if I knew how to work on foreign models, you'd think there were nothing but Volvos and Volks cramming up the streets.

And cab companies, I couldn't even get past the front desk. I guess they figured I was too young. Or maybe like Irv said, you have to slip the girl a buck in some of these places. He says you walk up to the desk with a five-spot in your hand, sort of folding it and messing with it, like it's some dirty old scrap of paper you're about to throw away. Then you get in to see somebody.

Fred said that was a lot of horsechips. Fred Breneman—this guy we were playing pool with, he said those girls out at the front desk don't pull any weight, and he ought to know—he's had jobs all over. He says you don't even know who to pay until you get inside and working. Then he says you better find out good, it's the only way you'll get ahead. Not that I believe him. Some places, they just pray. Mr. Meisner never would know enough to butter somebody to get ahead.

But that wasn't what had me stumped—it's how you get in. I wouldn't mind giving somebody a tip, only I'd like to know what I'm getting. One of these employment agency guys wanted this deposit—he wouldn't even tell me first if they had any jobs I could do. I guess I seemed kind of dense to him, I kept asking, well what kind of jobs did they have on their file? He finally told me to try State Employment if I wanted free entertainment. He gives me this little spit-on-you-smile—he was sore.

Telling me State Employment—he probably knew they're mostly working to get these poor people jobs. One look at my address. If I'd been a Negro, it would've been some help—there was a colored fellow from some organization, he was in conference with two of the State Employment guys, they were working something out for all the real poverty types, which I wished they'd ask me in on. Only obviously they didn't want any white people gumming it up.

When I finally did get to talk to a guy, I didn't fit into a classification. They've got their books arranged by experience. If you don't have any, they don't know what to feed into the computer to find out what you maybe might do. And like I said, if you're not really poor-off, they don't have time to fumble around.

Irv said I should've gone on and told them about the summer jobs. He said I could explain why I got fired. Like I could say the camp director was peculiar and made passes at me. Or the time at Ginnis and Clark, I could say one of the married women fell madly in love with me and I had to quit suddenly to avoid her getting into a scandal. Irv's got a great little imagination.

So Fred says, "Yeah, suppose you feed them a line and then they pull a lie-detector test on you?" I didn't know they could do that. I wouldn't even work for a place—they wire you up like a criminal, it really happened to Fred. He said he figured he could beat any cockeyed machine, you ought to be smarter than a bunch of bolts. So he said you keep breathing very evenly and you think about something else all the time—that louses the machine up. He thought about TV, like spacemen baloney which leaves him very cold. But it didn't work. Or anyhow he didn't get the job.

I should've skipped the doghouse that day, those guys. They were practically depressing.

Of course Irv was right about one thing, he said if I ever went and was a mechanic in some garage, he'd chop me dead. But I *told* him he was nuts to buy a car like a Buick with all those complicated guts he can't work on himself. He knows it, too. They charged him sixty bucks for repairs the other day and his motor still gags.

The trouble with him is, he's got plenty of money, he doesn't worry enough when he spends it. His old man owns a junkyard over north, there's a lot of money in junk. I told him, "It's O.K. for you to sit cool, you're going to take over the business someday. Everything turning to junk faster all the time, you've got it made."

So he says why don't I work for my father in the real estate racket? I told him a hundred times—it's no racket, not the way my father runs his firm. He won't handle any crummy houses that are going to fall down in a couple of years. He says there's plenty of good honest deals where you can make a buck. Anyway, I told Fred, "For your information, my father's got other guys to handle the customer relations." A whole gang, he calls them the "Fletcher-men." He never even *suggested* I should join up, I'll say that for him.

Oh, I know, he used to hustle clients himself, but he never conned anybody. It was more like he was being smart, like knowing a good horse trade. That's different. You sink your money in some investment that you figure will pay off when you sell it. It's sort of like gambling, except Pop doesn't approve of gambling. That's what gets me mixed up sometimes; like Nick used to say, "The risk is what makes the game tick."

If Nick had only been there that day, he'd know what was getting me all muddy. Since he got sent up, I don't know why I bother to go back to the place. And the law would pick that particular day to come sniffing around for minors. I shouldn't have mentioned it, forget I said it, huh? I wouldn't want to get the management in trouble, they kick in plenty for the message. You know, the call, the word —that there's going to be a check. So everybody under 21 can get gone, for the love of pete, *you* know.

Only that day we didn't know where else to go, to kill the rest of the afternoon. And Irv didn't exactly help. "Man," he says, "would I like to heave a rock right through their big, pretty, lousy front window." The Buick garage he was talking about. The only time I feel like being around Irv is when I wish I could kick the tail off somebody. Which is why I almost took him up—he said, why don't we go uptown and mess around?

But I hear myself telling him no thanks. Me and my conscience, I figure I've promised Doug about this supper thing. So I told him—Irv—I said I couldn't make it, I've got a date with this terrific girl I met at a coffee counter. How she's very sincere and stacked like a Barbie doll.

. . . .

Chicks . . . as Rion thought about it distantly, next morning . . . always turn into women, in the worst sense of the word. That nurse must have been somebody's dish once. Now her chin looked like it was carved out of a bar of Ivory. Of course you couldn't blame her, working in this place where all the crummy details of living are the big point. As if the only thing that matters is whether your body's clicking along on time. Who cares?

He was just as glad when the lawyer walked in. At least this guy could say "Hope you're feeling better" without it sounding like the Red Cross.

"Oh, I'm in great shape," Rion told him. "I had a ball all night last night—thinking about Mr. White's chart. He had this chart, to show how many more bucks you'll make if you graduate from high. Big deal, only I divided it up—years and months and weeks. So what good's a lousy ten-spot these days?"

"It can make the difference between that six-pack, the ball game, or a quiet evening at home with your fingernails," the lawyer said.

"Maybe. If you could get the kind of job his chart had in mind. Me, I should've stayed over north. Permanently. Get a room in some fleabag, you can always pick up a few pennies diving dishes. Come night, there's somewhere to spend it."

"You'd find the alleys can look very tired at seven o'clock the morning after. There's nothing more boring than to be poor."

"You keep sounding like Nick sometimes. Not

that money meant much to him. He used to say you can't eat it or wear it or waltz it around."

"But he took his risks for it."

"Because the game set him up. Every turn of the cards—he was living. If he'd wanted to get rich, he could've done a fast shuffle, like the sharks—better than anybody. But he wouldn't touch a stacked deck. What kick would that be, if you knew you were going to win every time?"

"And yet you have to make enough to stay in the game. To ante, to be able to call and raise, too. At least if you care about the long count, racked up in years."

"At the doghouse nobody worries past next Saturday night. Which is what you're driving at, I guess," Rion added.

The attorney gave him full score, with one of those approving looks. You hate yourself for caring what some old dodo thinks—at least until you remember that everybody else thinks you're nuts. One thing sure, he wasn't in business to give out a lot of sermons. Just curious, sometimes.

"Rion," he said, as if it just occurred to him, "how the devil did you get inside a place like that? Those dens don't exactly cater to the Cedar Woods crowd."

"You aren't kidding they don't. That's why I like it. That's why—" Rion hesitated to go into the details, but it was all part of the trip. "Right after that Ginnis and Clark deal, I don't know, I had to find out something. I couldn't just goof along at home. You wonder what the rest of the world's doing. Everybody always telling you—too young, for this and that. I didn't *feel* like some kind of a dumb kid, but I didn't know the score either—not any of it. So I kept looking, there wasn't a part of town I didn't cover last summer. Sooner or later you begin to smell where the action is."

"And you just strolled on in?"

"Well, I watched a while first—I knew some of those guys were no twenty-one. I noticed how they acted, sort of loose and careless. All the same, I was pretty nervous. It was a good thing the cashier got smart—when somebody's shirty, I build up inside. When he pulls this, about no minors allowed, I guess I made some crack because Nick wandered over—that's when I really got scared. He's a quiet-looking guy, not even very big, but he leaves no doubts. I knew I better not even begin to chicken, so I said, 'I was just asking how old you got to be to shoot a little pool here.' He says, 'Old enough to call your shots,' and hands me a cue."

"Wait a minute, you had played before?"

"Oh sure. Out at the Club we used to fool around until they put up the sign, no more juveniles in the game room. You don't think I'd go in a place if I didn't know how? But I was up so tight I could hardly get my breath. We went over to this table with the balls all scattered—there wasn't any setup for an easy shot, but I said, 'Six in the side.' And I put it there. 'Good thing,' Nick says, 'I had five bucks riding on you, Lefty.' He's the only guy ever made me feel like that."

Having spilled his entire guts, in spite of himself, Rion lay braced—any kind of crack, just any kind of crack . . .

But the attorney sat quiet as a man at a funeral.

Which didn't get them anywhere. At last Rion hitched up straighter against the pillows. "So I should've stayed there, that's all. At least I wouldn't be here, trying to climb out of this nice, high-class clean-type damn corner I'm in. Where were we?"

8

. . . .

I was on my way home for supper. Talk about
mistakes—I should *never* have swung for that. I
knew it, even on the bus. I sat next to some guy
carrying tools, I had to go start wondering. He certainly wasn't the type that knows people or tips
people. He didn't even bother to look out the window. And his tools, he didn't wrap up his plane—
the blade's jutting out, scraping against the saw and
all the other junk in his box. Mr. Giordello would
kill you if you ever treated a plane like that. So I

didn't ask him how he made the union. But I tell you, if there was one dinner I wished I didn't have to go to.

When I got home, Doug was standing inside ready to open the door for me. He must've been watching out the window. I scarcely walked in when he says, all happy, "Greetings, old buddy, Shirli's coping with the supper. How if I fix you a drink?" And he gives me this glass, it's pure ginger ale—not even a faint flavor in it.

I said, "As a bartender you'll make a great water commissioner," and I wasn't really kidding.

But he just smiled along. "How'd everything go today?"

I wasn't about to tell him everything stank, so I acted mysterious. I didn't feel like analyzing a whole lot of things. I hoped we could toss off the food and I could get out of there early, go to the Crossroads or somewhere. And in the meantime, Shirli should stick to her cooking. But I got a hint it wasn't going to be all that easy.

Underneath the smile, Doug's all in knots. Right away he starts muttering in my ear. "Between you and me, *I've* had a very rough day." He's been digging around in Shirli's complexes and you get the idea it came up slightly crackerjack. At least he says, "Don't be surprised if she's in a bit of a mood."

"What's she sore about now?" I asked.

"Oh, nothing really. I mean, she's a lovely feminine bundle of contradictions—she has a sort of logic that's horribly illogical. A wild idealism—well, I haven't got anything against that. But I tried to tell her, when you get married, responsibility rears its ugly head. I shouldn't have put it that way —played right into her hands, of course." He's practically talking to himself, trying to figure where he went wrong, which with a chick like her, you can't.

"Who won?" I asked.

"Oh, I let it go—I gave in. That's a necessary part of the courting syndrome," he says. I remember that word, because it made me think of the Rollerdrome and how it would be if you added a little sin. Which isn't what it means, I know that.

Anyhow I'm betting the babe is in a great little mood. I said, "How about if I bug off and let you two fight it out?"

"We are not fighting. We're experiencing each other," he tells me. "We need to frame ourselves in normal everyday situations. When we were at school everything was different, nothing seemed completely real—all very heady and stimulating. Her little quirks fell into place. I can't think what's gone wrong since we've come here into—" He meant the living world, crummy old life is what he meant. "It just takes some adjustment, that's all. That's the whole secret of being happy."

It always gripes me when people talk about happy. Especially since he looked like a guy who's trying to laugh it up when he just busted a thumb.

"Listen," I asked him, "what good is college if it leaves you so loused up you have to get over it?"

"That's not what I said." He goes on, sort of vague, "But you need to apply what you've learned. Everything has *some* explanation, even your wildest emotions. You have to try to make sense—why that should strike her as so repulsive—?"

About then, I even felt kind of sorry for Shirli. Because some things don't look so great when you talk about them too much. You can't explain everything. Like the way it feels to let in the clutch. Or why a piece of rhythm hits you in the lower belly, or when you break off a pitch that hangs just right. If that's what he was trying to be sensible about, I wouldn't buy it either. Why should you try? To narrow stuff down? But that's beside the point.

The point was, Shirli was stripped—clear off the map, all right. No, I don't mean clothes, she was wearing something with big orange triangles all over it. And the smile she gave us when she came to stand in the doorway, I felt like we were going to be the main course.

What it was, was shrimp. Mom's best crystal punch bowl full of these shrimp with the legs still on. And a plate of anchovies laid out in a circle like they'd had it. Plus a dish of olives—she put them in a dish that Mom *always* uses for candied fruit, with a silver fork. Doug gives one look, and I know what he's thinking. Anyhow olives stuffed with white always seem wrong. I couldn't touch them myself.

He wasn't in too great shape either. Sort of waving his hands over the shrimp—there's only one way you can peel a dead shrimp, which is bare-handed. "Dear," he says, very head-of-the-house, "don't we need some container for the shells?"

"Oh, I forgot. Of course." She goes and gets this wicker basket that Mom uses, with a linen napkin, to serve hot bread in. "A casket for their poor little mortal remains."

Doug gives her a sickly look. "Don't you think your frame of reference is a bit gruesome?"

"Probably. There's probably some deep psychological clue to that." She nods around like she's trying to help. "Didn't Mr. Phillipson cover it? Maybe I've got a death wish. Or maybe it's latent schizo. Shall we yo-yo?" She goes right on passing the potato chips. "Rion," she says, "your brother has been trying—really struggling—to psychoanalyze me. Awfully thankless, I'm afraid, since the analyzee can hardly admit that he—or she—is a kook."

Doug winces, like ha-ha. "Nonsense, I was only trying to give us both a little perspective. So we can adjust—"

"Isn't that rare and stimulating?" Like before, she angles the words at me, but I was really only scenery. She says, "To think, when Doug and I first met we had so much silly fun *not* being adjusted. I suppose that's life, though. Rion, when you race with that little friend of yours out there, when you're running with the wind, do you ever stop to adjust her carburetor?"

"Damn right," I said, "if you want good mileage."

I guess that wasn't the right answer. She turns her telescopic sights on me, going to give me the old business. "Oh-Rion, you look scorched. As if you'd walked down into Dante's cut-rate inferno today. What level did you reach? At least you didn't wait to read the news from Milton—who was blind anyhow. In college you pick up this little gossip."

For her information we weren't completely ignorant in high school English. I said, "Me, I get my laughs from Beowulf."

Sort of startled her, she liked it. "One of my favorites. All about monsters who can tear a man's arm out by the roots. Blood so hot it will melt a sword—wait'll you get to college and some anemic fool asks you to scan the meter. By the time they get through briefing you on life and death and love, you won't be *able* to go down into the beautiful fierce flames yourself. You won't have the poop." And she gives Doug a sweet smile.

So I said, "Well, if you mean like downtown, I'd just as soon skip it. It was hot as ten stoves today." And Doug looked like he could kiss my hand.

"How did it go," he asks me, turning a shoulder to her, "whatever it was you were off to, this morning? On the level, if you'd hang around at home a while we could work out some ideas I have that might be of use to you next fall. At whatever school you decide on. Freshman year is really the foundation for a lot of important things that come later. Not just classwork but, for instance, pledging a frat. Not that I'd twist your arm, but it's definitely an asset."

Shirli laughs, "Oh-ha-ha-ha-ha-ha-*ha*. Yes indeed, it's like the Christian religion to some campus types. Either you belong or you don't have a right to walk the earth. I'm afraid I'm a disbeliever myself—I never told you, old pickle, I got alienated from my sisterhood last spring. Remember when the whole little nunnery went to Fort Lauderdale? I couldn't take it—I walked out across the beach at dawn, stepping over the dead bodies. Everybody sound asleep. At *dawn*. On Easter. So I threw my sorority pin in the ocean and shaved my head, and ever since, I've walked the earth carrying a lantern in one hand, looking for a man. I'm beginning to think Socrates was asking too much when he expected honesty too."

She thought she was going over my head, and all it was, she's feeling a little sorry for herself, which I never am too strong on, when they pull it. I said, "You got nothing to cry about. You did O.K.—you and Doug'll make a great match." Only he wasn't helping much, sitting there picking the legs off the shrimp like that.

Shirli gives him a look, her face all tied up. "What good is a match if it doesn't burn?" she says, laughing or not laughing again. "Even friction doesn't seem to work. But then who'd ever try to persuade a match that it wasn't made to light fires? Of course you *can*. You can pour cold water all over the poor little thing. With human beings, it's more complicated."

Doug doesn't usually get red in the face, especially at the table he can always change the subject to food. But not that night.

"I don't care, dear pickle," she goes on, "it does get complicated. Ask anybody who works in an insane asylum—the orderlies will tell you. It's hard to save people from their own passions. Their lovely exciting, vivid rebellions and desires, their anger and their wildness—all their fire, in other words. They have to get tough. They strap you to the bed, or wrap you in a sheet so you can't move a muscle and lay you in a tepid bath. For hours," she informs me. "They don't care if you cry. They're used to that."

. . . .

Rion felt that swell of sickness come over him again —the whole memory of it heaved inside him. Her talking along in that casual way, like a surgeon gabbing about somebody's kidneys. And crunching the potato chips.

"Sir," he said to the lawyer, "you probably know. Do they really pull that kind of stuff? I mean when you're socked away for treatment?" He kept thinking of the neat phony words his parents used— professional help, they called it. "And some of the other stuff Shirli told about, how they rig you up with electrodes and shock all the guts out of you. Or shoot you with tranquilizers so you go quietly and be good for the rest of your life."

The attorney shoved his lower lip out and shook his head, but not much. "I'd say Shirli was over-dramatizing. By the way, what was Doug's reaction?"

"I don't know. Something—how she should go ahead and get it out of her system. He was being patient and so forth, but what it was doing to my system! I didn't even feel like going out to Cross-roads. As for this advice he was supposed to give me, we *both* forgot about that. All I did was, I hit the sack. It wasn't more than nine o'clock. I thought I was tired, after the night before at the gravel pit, but after I got in bed, I was either hot or I was cold. When I did drop off, I kept having cold dreams—some girl with pink hair. We were all floating around in the river and I kept trying to explain why we ought to get out. She was a real clean-looking girl . . . well, you don't want to hear about that."

9

. . . .

When I woke up it was still only about midnight. I could hear them talking downstairs and some weird music going. That Russian that Doug likes, I forget —not Tchaikovsky, something freakier, yeah, Stravinsky. About this Firebird, which made me wonder who's getting to who, all that yak-yak going on and the music whistling around. If he's digging in her complexes to the tune of that!

The next time I woke up, I heard him close the garage doors and tiptoe on upstairs. He'd taken her back to her aunt, I guess. Only I wondered what *he* got out of the evening. Was it some sort of kick, to let her slice away at him? Maybe it's sophisticated, the way you get in college. It kept sneaking up on me, the whole idea—hanging there over my left shoulder along with that traffic ticket and a few other things I didn't want to think about. Anyhow I couldn't get my eyes closed.

I remember it starting to get light—we've got robins around. I guess there really were some woods in the neighborhood once—not cedar, I don't think. That's how my mind kept going. And when I finally did drift under, I didn't come up for air until about noon. I saw that clock, and I thought—it sounds lousy, but I thought—good! It's too late to do anything today. I never used to feel that way, like I wished I didn't ever have to get out of bed. I was still feeling those shrimps, I guess.

Doug, too. When I went down, he's sitting in the kitchen with all the dirty dishes. He gave me a kind of grin, it was exactly right all at once—him and me. I began to feel better. He poured me some coffee. "Did you sleep it off, the dinner?" he asks.

"Maybe when the coffee takes hold," I told him.

"If it's any comfort, I got pretty firm with her after you left. All that act," he says, "she takes refuge in a peculiar whimsy—it's like a protective coloring. When she's frightened by a situation, she retreats behind this spotty humor. And right now, she's pretty upset. I'd better tell you, we never have been really engaged. The reason I invited her here was to convince her—that she's not so different from everybody else in the world. That it wouldn't be impossible for her to settle down and want some security and lead a warm, interesting kind of life like Mother does. She'd find it very fulfilling, once she got used to it. I've tried to get her to *feel* like Mother. I simply must—that is a necessity. To my life, anyhow."

I never heard Doug talk so personal before, right *to* me. It nearly flipped me, him being so honest about it.

"So did you get it cleared up last night?" I asked.

"I hope so. She seemed sorry that she'd made you the whipping boy for her frustration. After you left, she almost seemed about to cry. I wish Phillipson were here, I'm not as good at this as he is." He tried to fill me in on it, how you've got to try to understand your own hang-ups. Like take him, he knows exactly why he's hooked on Shirli.

"She's the exact opposite of everything I am—she's rare and impulsive and brave," he says, "but there are some unresolved problems I've got to help her with. She doesn't seem to realize that her romantic side has to come down to earth. People are *people*." For instance, he tells me, "She has a curious reaction to you—I thought it was maternal instinct, but since last night I think she's over-romanticizing again. You're a challenge—she's trying to win out over your antagonism. Excuse me, old buddy, but it's been pretty obvious from the beginning that you don't like her." And then he says, "Do you? Doesn't she appeal to you physically?"

I didn't tell him she'd *tried* appealing to me physically. I should've—it was an opening. But the truth was, he all at once looked suspicious. Of me.

Anyhow, I usually steer clear when it comes to giving anybody advice on their love life, it's got no future. So I let it go, how she's probably a great kid when you get to know her—I forget what I said. Something. I didn't want to seem like I really didn't like her, so I guess I said she was a real unusual girl, that's always safe. The only thing, I said, she's a little bit over my head.

That made him get all relieved for some reason. "Exactly. Which is why you need the benefit of keen minds—" Going on about college, and wisdom, for cornsake! What he was getting at was the maturity angle—he said I needed more of it. Which if he only knew.

"Don't you realize," he tells me, "that the whole future of the nation depends on those of us who learn to control the patterns of human behavior? Think of the consequences when top executives make decisions—" I don't know, something about how the whole economy depends on their inner factors. Like the country might fall apart if the president of GM doesn't have his factors in shape when he O.K.'s a new-model Chevy.

"So all right," I said. "But where do *you* get on board? You can't just walk into some outfit and say, 'I'd make a great president, my factors are plugged in—take me, I'm yours.'"

Doug gives me a funny look. He kept walking up and down—you know the way your toes don't track when you can't make up your mind? Says, "For me, it's got to be some key position—possibly in personnel. The man who guides the payroll today may shape policy tomorrow. Dealing with the human raw materials . . ." This is something he read in a book somewhere. "Anyhow, that is exactly why I have to go on with my education—I don't see why she can't understand it," he mumbles. "I'm doing it for her sake. I thought she'd be keen to—help me along." Poor guy, he's saved up his allowance, he says, and there's enough for them both to go back to school for another year, which should help her get *her* factors glued down. He's so serious about it.

But I can't do it, I *can't* look like something sounds wonderful when it doesn't. I told him, "That's tricky stuff, digging around, explaining too much. Remember Mr. White? He was an absolute nut on emotions, he was always talking about some balance-wheel you have to keep in control. And if you ask me, he didn't have enough sense to put between his two toes."

"There's no need to get crude," he snaps. "White's a very *fine* man." Just the way Mom always says it.

I started to change the whole subject, but damn, I sure didn't want Doug turning out like that. I said, "Maybe he was real brilliant before he had to go and be an adviser and adjust everybody—"

"Someday"—Doug begins pointing at me the way he knows I hate—"you'll wish you'd listened to him. You could *use* a little sense of responsibility."

"What's responsibility? So I did like he told me, I took Latin, and if that wasn't a bust—"

"You're being childish!" he yells.

"O.K., so excuse me if it's childish when I don't care about being bored to death."

Jeez, that set him off. "*Bored?* Oh, you'll change that tune. Just wait till you find yourself in the middle of the competition in a university today. Even State—it will be a miracle if you don't get washed out your first semester."

State was a new idea. I never thought of that. It's not as hard to get in as some others, because it's tax-supported, and Doug's ready to help. Tells me how he's been developing the idea all day, had some people on the phone. I'll have to take entrance exams, but he'll help me get in shape. Talking in this sorrowful kind of way, like I'm almost a lost cause, but he forgives me. I felt about the size of a bus token—I even began to wash the dishes.

"Tonight," he says, "a friend of mine is coming over to discuss it—you may remember him from high school, Norm Ashburn?" A big hero, year ahead of Doug—basketball, track, football, all that. Now he's on some alumni committee for State and he might know how to get me in there. If I could prove I was in earnest and so forth. "So please put on some decent clothes and do me one favor," he says. "This evening, will you *please* try to control yourself in front of Shirli?"

. . . .

The lawyer looked out over the tops of the bifocals, about to say something.

Rion made a random thrust with his fingers that left his lanky hair in peaks. "I don't know what he was driving at. I swear, I never got uncontrolled with that chick, not even later. All I could figure, he's got nerves on top the nerves."

"There's something else I wanted to shake out a little. You told me the other day you'd definitely decided not to go to college—"

"Aw hell, you don't *decide*. Not off the top of your head, the way I was talking around that other morning. All I knew was, I hadn't exactly made a great name for myself out looking for a job, and if somebody else knew a few ropes, well, it couldn't hurt to listen. Of course I wasn't crazy about Shirli being in on the deal, but if it'll help her fundamental— That's what Doug called it. 'She has all the fundamental charm to be a beautiful hostess.' So O.K., but no more shrimp, I told him that flat. I will go out to The Diner for a fast hamburger and be back by eight o'clock. He knew I meant it too. All he said was to be on time, because this Ashburn's a well-heeled type, got a good position and a house over in Melanie Hills and Doug hopes I will rise to the occasion. Some way to start an evening."

10

· · · · · · · · · ·

That's why I got this hunch I should have a hold on
something, some idea of my own in case the other
angles went soft. You like to feel you've got some
solid ground to fall back on. So as soon as I got to
The Diner, I bought an evening paper. There were
a couple of ads: Wanted to train. Sounded like more
Ginnis and Clark. But there was one that had possi-
bilities—the telephone company was looking for
guys who were draft-exempt. And I'm 1-Y, don't ask
me how. Or else ask my father, I guess, I don't want
to think about it.

But telephones didn't sit too sour—linemen, it's pretty risky stuff. Go right out there with the lightning cracking, you got to pin the wires back up. People might be dying. Anyhow, tomorrow I could look into it. After that, I didn't mind so much heading home. You know, you need to feel you're under your own power.

I didn't even mind when Doug's waiting for me to come up from the garage. Asks would I *kindly* go put on a tie, and hurry up, they're here. Well, he's right—I'm not too great when it comes to etiquette. I wasn't irked, I just asked him if he'd fix me a drink I could taste for a change—the heat wave was really coming on that night. Air felt like right off the Devil's bathtub.

Doug kind of moans. "If you're going to be crude—"

I almost told him I'd take my crude lousy self to an air-conditioned movie, but I didn't. I remembered he's having trouble with the babe, she's probably the one not being civilized. If she showed up in a topless bikini I wouldn't have blinked.

She didn't, but it was almost worse. When I came into the living room—I didn't know this Norm Ashburn was married—the two girls are sitting there like the execution is about to take place. His wife, Betty, she's a pretty type, the kind that wears blue dresses and white gloves and a little gold pin. Some sorority—I forget—like Theta Beta or something.

Shirli's sitting in this straight chair with her knees crossed, in this tight black dress—on anybody else it would have looked like a mummy. Buttoned clear up to the chin—linen, I think. On her, it was sexy as hell—maybe because her arms hung out bare. I don't know how anybody's arms could look that naked. Talking along friendly, friendly, to this Betty.

"I had a roommate who was a Theta Beta. In fact I always *admired* the Theta Betas for pledging her," she says. "Once you got to know her, she had a lovely soul."

Betty looks at Norm like, what did you get me into here?

But he keeps right on grinning. I think when he was a college all-star he did a few ads for some razor company. He's glad to know me and all that, and what position do I play? He meant football. I told him, I never went out for the team. I had enough troubles without some coach leaning on me—not that I said that, of course. I said I was too light to make it or something.

He says, nonsense, I'd make a great lineman.

So—I don't know why, just talking along—I said, "That's about what I've got in mind. I'm going down to the telephone company tomorrow and see about it. They're looking for men—you know, climb the poles, keep things tight along the line." I was laughing it up, for cornsake. Then I saw the look on Doug's face, like I'd just announced I was about to become an unwed father. I had to go on. "The truth is, I figure it's kind of too late for me to try growing an egghead." And that wasn't the right approach either.

Doug mumbles around, something about "Don't mind the kid, he's full of the old spirit—anxious to get out and butt up against life." He was trying to cover for me.

Shirli's the only one really keeping her balance. On that chair, it's a narrow chair that everybody hates. And this cigarette barely caught in her fingers, the ash getting longer and longer. She doesn't move a muscle, she just looks at Doug. "Did you ever try it? Butting your head up against life, I mean?"

"That's rather a snide question," he answers, with another one of those ha-ha laughs.

"But it can be dangerous," she says. "Take that buffalo up in Yellowstone Park. He butted—a tourist who was taking his picture. So they destroyed him, they gave his meat to the Indians. His young, strong, tender loins. And the Indians will let you take their picture for a lousy buck."

You could've filed your nails on the silence. Then Doug comes back—like I said, when there's company you can hardly stump him. "Poor devil"—he laughs along—"at least they might have sent his ribs down to Jackson Hole where he'd have made history in a gourmet restaurant."

Shirli gave him a smile, a real smile. She liked that. "I'll have to think, whether I'd prefer to be eaten in great ugly gulps by the poor? Or delicately seasoned and delivered up to some millionaire's banquet at ten dollars a plate."

All this is sort of beyond the Ashburns. Norm's smile didn't even dim. He said, "Well, you can always go out for track, old boy." Meaning me.

And Doug jumps on. "Sure, sure." How I've just got a slight inferiority thing about college, but that's what alumni are for, to show the younger types the way.

Norm didn't get it, but Betty did. She says, "Oh absolutely, Rion. You'll find college so enriching—you meet so many people with bright questioning minds—that's the main thing about school, the atmosphere."

"Do you think so?" Shirli—and if she's an example, I can only picture her enriching me in exactly one way. "Of course, maybe the atmosphere is better at State," she says. "On our campus, we had a smog problem. The air was thickest over the psychology lab—every time Mr. Phillipson lectured we had a red alert."

About then, Doug is almost losing *his* id. He laughs like, shut up, will you? "To be serious for a minute—"

"I'm completely serious," Shirli says. "I want Rion to go on to deeper things as much as you do, pickle. I'll never forget my first intellectual crisis. I had to do a term paper on T. S. Eliot right when I'd had my conversion to Zen." She turns to Betty very earnestly. "When did you have your first religious experience?"

Betty jumped like somebody pinched her elbow. "I'm an Episcopalian," she says.

"Shirli, dear"—Doug is really getting sore—"your humor is a little exotic, dear. And speaking of Eliot, remember that poem he wrote? About the fellow *who murdered his girl friend?*"

Shirli brightens right up. "Of course! He kept her body in the bathtub and locked the door. Every day he looked out the window at the people passing by, he thought—if they were alive, then he was dead. Didn't you ever wonder the same," she asks, "say, when you watch Rion go out of here in his hot rod?"

I could've slid between the cracks, her calling it a hot rod. Doug was pretty thin, too, because she ends up, "Rion, if you ever kill your mistress, don't do it by degrees"—she says this very ladylike—"stick the knife right in her guts."

Well, Doug said he was going to fix us a drink and Norm said he'd help, and I sure wasn't going to get left in there with the females—I didn't feel *that* sorry for Betty. Besides, my last drink, I don't know what he made it out of but it tasted like half Coke and half root beer.

When we got out in the kitchen, old Norm didn't waste time, he slugged himself right out of the bottle of V.V.O.—he's pretty much past being in any shaving ads these days. He did apologize for doing it so quick. Seems he had a hard day at the office.

I've been trying to remember—something took a turn that night, out there in the kitchen. Only I'm not sure what. Doug and Norm did most of the talking. They kind of forgot about me and the college angle—all Norm does for State is recruit for their football team once in a while, which it's no wonder State never wins anything if you ask me.

Mainly he's up to his ears in bigger stuff—something about midsummer promotion and the advertising budget. You could tell he thought it was a big deal.

So I asked him, "What line are you in?"

"Glister," he says. You know the stuff, it's a wax or something, on TV you see these babies crawling around on the floor. Anyhow he's with Glister, like it's the secret service. Doug gives me a dirty look, but I couldn't help it.

I did try to act interested. "What sort of job?"

That's when he says, "In production management —I'm a coordinator."

I guess I did another take, because Doug gets *very* thin in the nose. But Lord, I happened to know a coordinator once. It was down at camp, he was in charge of activities. His job was to come around, we'd be right in the middle of an inning, and he'd break it up so we should go on a nature walk or something. He busted up the kids' games because that's what *time* it was.

Only I couldn't explain it right then to Doug. And I knew he'd be sore if I said good night, I'm sleepy, which was the truth. So after I got back from taking the girls their drinks, I settled into the scenery while he and Norm bulled around. I was hardly listening until it dawned on me all of a sudden, Norm was hinting about a touch.

No small touch, either—he needs five hundred bucks, something about repairs on his garage. I thought those houses in Melanie Hills were built solid. At least Pop never includes them when he talks about urban renewal, which is how he jokes about new junk developments. But the land's been shifting under Norm's foundation, and he's in pretty deep for his new car, he says, you got to keep up appearances when you're in a sensitive position. Doug hedged out of that corner pretty neat, saying he had to conserve all his funds for this postgraduate work he's planning.

Norm laughs his jaw out of joint, he was a little peeved at the turndown. "When they offer a master's in the art of spreading the old butter," he says, "then it might be worth your time."

Doug's chuckling around, a certain way he has when he's strangling to be polite. "Hell, boy," he says, "don't you know—industry's thirsting for men with expertise. The more advanced program you've followed, the better the job."

"Depends, depends." Norm keeps nursing the bottle. "How long can you afford to fool around? You hide out on campus long enough, you better stay there until you can apply for social security and skip the rest. Glister doesn't even look at your application if you're over thirty." He explained about insurance and pensions, I don't remember it all.

But it was news to Doug. "Why, man, you can't *get* a Ph.D. properly before you're thirty," he says. "I doubt if the actuarial tables rule out good key personnel. What I expect to skip is a lot of grubwork —I'm going for the higher stratosphere."

"The air's pretty rare up there." Norm's feeling no pain by now. He sees me wheeling past his head, he says, "Riley, you got the right idea. With those phone poles, I mean. Back roads—keep on the move—I was going to be a trucker myself once. Gonna shove a big rig—every long haul in this old country, road signs comin' at you in the headlights and nobody riding the tailgate." He squints at Doug. "And speaking of wives, that little babe of yours— she'd climb aboard a diesel in a minute. You got lucky there, Doug, old kid. You'd never have to worry about her feeling the bumps—hell, she'd spell you at the wheel."

Doug's very sober, he isn't even touching the drinks now. "Shirli is a bit bohemian, of course, but it's only a phase."

"She's a hot one with the phrases," Norm says, all tickled. "You got a good thing going, don't tame 'er down too much. What the devil, you got no boss coming home to dinner tomorrow night. Let 'er rip!" He whoops around—it was all we could do to steer him on back into the front room. With Doug talking fast, to cover up all the sloshing around, telling Betty that Norm's got a dizzy spell and can she make it home O.K.?

He didn't waste much time getting Shirli on the

road, either. They all went out together. After they were gone, there I was with a bunch of stale glasses and the whole house all around me. I did take the girls' drinks out to the kitchen, I can't stand that sort of sad scenery. Then I gathered up what was left of the V.V.O. and went back in and sat down in Pop's chair—I even wiped the rings off the coffee table.

I thought, O.K., I am nowhere. Thank the Lord. Just a room, like one I never saw before, it could be any place. The curtains are always pulled across our picture window, who knows what's outside? Or where the streets lead off to or whether it's day or night. Just me and the old bottle. I took a good big jolt of it straight, and for a minute I thought I didn't have any stomach.

The second slug loosened my knees, and I wondered when do you start to feel good? I never went in for anything stronger than beer, it's too damned expensive and I never cared that much. So I tried again—all that happened was, everything skidded slightly like the horizontal focus was off. Maybe if I'd kept with it.

But about then, I had to go and think about Nick. He always said a guy would have to be dumb, to short out the connections to his own brain. Your mind's all you got going for you. He wouldn't even touch three-two, at least I never saw him take a drink of anything stronger than coffee. You'd have to know him. Because you might think it meant he was weak or something—nobody I ever knew could even cut decks with him. If I could've talked a little to him right then—I swear I thought of putting in long distance to the Federal pen. That's where they've got him. Well, I told you that, didn't I?

· · · · · · · · · ·

Rion stared away toward the window. The afternoon had taken a turn into sundown. Over on the north side, the lights would be spurting—patches of red neon and yellow and blazing white, up and down the face of the old city. Music from a jukebox, sometimes raw and cool—they don't spin those disks, the jocks don't, not over the public airways. With the lazy bitter lyrics, cutting through the waves of heat. The slap of cards on a table, everybody's shirt soaked—smoke smell and short words, shoving the excitement up. Don't have to think— you just feel and that's enough.

Or is it? Rion went slack against the sterilized sheets. All at once, as if something had pulled the plug, he felt drained. What it was, of course—he was stalling. Trying to put off telling about the end of that evening.

11
· · · · · · · · · ·

Did you ever notice how something happens to a house about midnight—like the light bulbs stare at you? I've felt it before when I was alone in the living room, only this time it didn't let up when I heard Doug drive in. The garage door didn't even squeak the way it does. I could hardly hear him coming down the hall. And when he stood there in the door —you know, it can seem kind of weird, somebody stares at you.

He finally came over and took the bottle and

poured some in a glass—like they say, he tossed it off. Which would've looked greater to me if I hadn't already tried it myself. Or maybe it was the way he took over the fireplace—that's where Pop always stands when he wants to hold forth. Doug wiggles his rump, he could've practically given Pop lessons. He can get like that, and right then I was in no mood.

"You were great tonight," he says, "absolutely great. Our son, the telephone repairman."

"Old Norm didn't think it was so crazy," I mentioned.

"Old Norm," he says, "is too far gone to think anything. When the Russians compute their potential overkill, they can revise their estimates—it would only take half the usual dose to push Norm over and his little Betty is pure gravy. Good Lord, I hate a pleasant girl. Oh, it was a mistake to ask them," he says, almost like he's happy to admit it. But the Ashburns weren't really the point—he's practically turning blue over something else.

So, I don't know what gets into me—I knew I was walking into it—I said, "I thought Betty seemed real civilized."

"Mm-hm." He nods, you could hardly hear him the house was so quiet. "You're making sport of what I said earlier, aren't you? I've just begun to realize what's been going on, how you've been needling me lately."

"Nah," I told him, "forget it. All I meant was sometimes people *can* get along and even be more interesting when they are slightly crude. Old Norm may have good manners, but I noticed he didn't learn when he's had enough down the hatch. I bet he never learned to figure the odds, or how to size up a long shot or spot a fink—"

"Oh yes, we all suspected you've made some curious associations this past year." Doug smiles like tolerantly, except he couldn't get his lips to work right. "You think Father isn't aware of your rambling all over the city? I told him he was being too permissive—you've obviously picked up some hairy bedfellows."

"You don't know anything about my bedfellows, and don't say anything against my friends either," I told him, "because if I never meet any more of yours—" What came across my mind was, it was nobody's business but mine if I wanted to be a lineman or a grease monkey or honorary beekeeper. "These types that are going to enrich my life, you can give them back to Glister and let them coordinate everything in sight."

"Oh, you made that very obvious. In fact you've been completely free with your insinuations tonight, sneering at eggheads, and the way you lapped up Shirli's little jokes about learning. Just the most sacred gift we've got, that's all—the thing that separates the eagles from the worms. You're so worried about being bored, you might find out that a contest of minds can be rather fierce, even thrilling. It only shows how basically misguided you've become—to confuse muscle with strength, and mistake recklessness for courage."

"O.K., O.K.," I said at last. "Forget about the telephone business, it's not nailed down yet anyhow."

He poured himself another drink. "Well, at least that's something to be thankful for."

There he is, being relieved that I'm giving up something maybe I really wanted, how did he know? And right then it hit me, that we weren't kids any more, pretending a lot of stuff about what we'd do when we were grown. We're here. It didn't make me feel too good, I don't know why.

I said, "What it is, I guess we've kind of changed some, we need to get some new signals."

"Oh you've changed, all right." He's halfway talking to himself. "Father said you had, but I'm only now realizing the extent of the damage."

"Damage?" That gigged me all over again.

"What influences *have* been at work on you?" He gives me this leery look. "To turn you against me?

We were always pretty good friends, I thought. At least you never tried to belittle me. And in front of *her*—"

By then I really didn't know what he was talking about.

"Don't act so innocent!" he shouts all at once. "That remark of hers about your souped-up pile of junk, you think I didn't get it? I saw you two together down in the driveway the other evening, whispering around."

"Well, then you saw me cut on out of there too. What's the beef? You think I *like* her? I can't stand her!" I didn't mean to say it like that, he kind of shivers. "Buddy," I told him, "I never spoke two kind words to that chick—not on purpose anyhow. If she latched onto anything I said, she's writing her own script."

He kept looking a little dizzy, he didn't need any more V.V.O. Talking along to himself. "All the way home, she kept laughing—that way she laughs. Making up a terrible little fairy tale, about how we'd have to be married by computer—we'd ask it to be godfather to our children. Name them things like Project One and Secondary Plan. Except the youngest—she'd like to call him Nonformulated, he'd be the rebel of the family. He'd be allowed real food once a week, we could even touch him after sanitizing our hands. The others would be raised on concentrates in a sterile chamber. Other things—I couldn't repeat," he says in this weird little voice. Well, he was sloshed, and it was too late to have all those lights on. I'd have given every cent in the bank to get out of there, but I couldn't just leave him.

"Why should she try to make me ashamed of my intellect?" he says. "As if I'm afraid to grapple with life—oh, I know she was daring me to lose my self-control. But what's left, if you don't have control? I'm *glad* I've got some sense of decency, you'd think she'd be grateful. Or at least have a little mercy—"

"Women don't, none of 'em. Take it easy," I kept telling him.

But he didn't hear much by then. "I tried to explain to her how if I'm being conservative, it's to assure her future, *her* security. You have to move slowly— And she turned on me. 'How long has it been since you counted time by the beat of your heart?' she cried. 'Go ask your brother about that—he knows!'"

Well, anyhow, I finally got him up to his room. I hoped he was going to forget about the whole thing, some stuff it doesn't pay to remember. And I thought it was going to be O.K. After a while I heard him put some records on. But then I wasn't

122 . . .

too sure—the music was that German guy, Wagner. I can always tell when it's him, it makes you feel like you should commit suicide. Strictly from hunger.

. . . .

With a lot of new sunlight coming down on the foot of the bed that next morning, Rion felt better. He wished they could get this over with now. "Listen," he told the lawyer, "nothing happened that whole next day—it didn't get anywhere, so can we skip it?"

"Oh, it got somewhere." The attorney shuffled his papers and found the one he was looking for. "Just to keep the record straight, you got as far as City Hall Park."

"How the hell—? Excuse me, sir, only how did you hear about that? The cop didn't arrest me or anything."

"No, but he recognized you later, at the station, and added his two-bits' worth to your file. Seems to point to some sort of emotional disturbance, so you'd better square it if you can."

"There's nothing to square!"

The attorney settled himself to wait.

"Aw, damn it, sir, I can't tell all that, it's too stupid."

"Look, Rion. If your friend Nick were here, I've an idea he'd say 'Go with the whole story—don't forfeit the game, Lefty.'"

It caught Rion up sharp, because it sounded so true. "Funny, he's the only one ever called me that. He said I was the first left-handed billiard player he ever saw that was any good. Billiards was his game—he taught me. He showed me how most guys, if they can't score, they'll try to leave you out of position for a right-handed shot. But left-handed you can cream it. It always set him up, trying to think left-handed when he was playing me. They—nobody—could ever turn him off. I bet he's sitting up there in his cell right now, making book on the cockroaches. I wish I was with him."

The lawyer didn't look shocked. "And yet if he's half the man you say, he wouldn't want that."

"No. He always said I should stick with school. He used to get real tough about it—he said it was his world I was going to be running someday, young guys like me. You hear people talk like that, but he made me feel I might. Crazy, how he'd discuss stuff with a kid, a mixed-up dope of a kid—it was like a hobby to him. And listen? He could listen in all four gears. Boy, those billiard games we had—and yet he could've been sent up for that, just for treating me like I'm old enough to be human. Can you figure it? I can't—I don't even get some damn *little* law that says it's a crime to lie down on the grass on a hot day."

"Is that why you gave the patrolman a hard time? He said you almost got violent."

"Where'd he dream that up? Or did I maybe—I don't know. O.K. I'll try to lay the whole thing out, maybe it did add up to the final score."

12

. . . .

All the way in to the bus station that morning I tried to talk sense. I kept saying, "Get off, you complete jerk, now before it's too late." And all the time I kept right on sitting there. You can get like that, some fool idea gets a grab on you.

I told myself, she's fat, she probably eats like a baby elephant, and besides, there are one million lonesome chicks in the world if you need to talk to somebody, and no danger you might get to liking them too much. So what do I do? I turn up looking at myself in the same mirror in the washroom, putting on the tie and wishing I didn't forget to shave. I used to only need a shave every other day. And that morning I was so busy getting out without Doug hearing me, I didn't realize how my jaw had quite a nap on it. But I didn't let it stop me—when I get hooked on something.

When I sat down at the counter, she gave me one of those clean looks, coffee without me even asking. I damn near cried in my cup. I didn't care if she weighed *three* hundred. All the time she was cooking up food for the others—the counter was pretty busy—I kept watching her reverse view and practically falling in love with it. I thought, a double feature at the Drive-in, and then I ruled that out. I wouldn't want her to think what most girls would think if you mentioned a drive-in movie on the first date. Besides, she might be pretty innocent, I thought she probably never *went* to a drive-in with a guy.

What I mostly wanted was to talk, you could tell she'd be interested. So maybe we should go out to the Crossroads, except Irv and the guys might come in. Not that I'd care what they think, but she might size *them* up. Anyhow a girl like that would get more kick out of dressing up and maybe go dance a little at some of the three-two spots. She was light on her feet—I thought you could teach her anything.

And when she did get back to me, she had a little scoop of hair coming loose down the back of her neck. I didn't even know how I wanted my eggs. I said, I kept reading the menu, "I'll take number seven."

So she smiles all up. "Who you kidding?" Because there wasn't any number seven.

"That's the one where I pick you up at your place, like seven tonight if you're not busy." I thought it'd be only polite to pretend she might be.

"Why honey, that's nice," she says. "And thanks a million, I'm sorry I can't. The fact is—the management doesn't know, it's against rules—but I'm married."

Why is it, if somebody's married they have to tell you all about it? How her husband's a tire salesman, only they're getting out of the old rut—she's working to help pay off the trailer they live in and then they're going to Alaska. All that, I got while I'm trying to somehow eat a few eggs. She did ask me what work I was in, and I told her telephones. She thought it was great, she really did.

I forgot to mention I called about the ad. What they wanted was clerks for their billing department.

So that was that, and the rest of the day, ditto.

Those application blanks—four pages long, how can they think of that many questions? I mean, I don't even know what my father's annual income is, and if I did, I should tell them? Listen, what right have they got to ask if your parents ever had any serious illnesses, what business is that? And one of them—what goals did I set for myself? I almost put down, "I have a swinging ambition to rob a bank."

Only you could see that these personnel guys got no sense of humor. It's not their fault—they just couldn't have. A sense of anything. They're too neat, always sort of smiling, but at the same time you can see 'em drift.

Well, one guy did tap his pencil a minute like he was really trying to remember if they had some very small type job open that I might do. And of course it was hot—all of them in these dark suits. I don't hold it against them if they didn't give me the time of day.

But the later it got, the more I thought, what the hell? Especially that last deal—I never should've gone there. I knew something was fishy, the ad was in the paper three days in a row, I noticed it. Man wanted for warehouse job, no experience necessary. Plenty of guys around to grab something like that, unless it's the kind of place where they break your back for you.

Loading furniture, I figured, but so what? That stuff Norm mentioned about trucking made me think—how a trucker gets around and all. Maybe end up with a fleet of your own. So it might be a chance to get to know a few drivers, working on a freight dock. They could fill you in—there must be some kind of knack you can sign up with the Teamsters. Guys do it.

But as soon as I got there—it wasn't too early, about three in the afternoon—I saw this bunch of fellows hanging around the door of the hiring office. The way they looked at me, I should've saved my time. But I went on in and let the guy at the desk give me the brush-off. "Come back tomorrow, something may open up," which was the kind of deal it was.

When I went out again, one of the fellows hollers over, "Come join us in prayer. We're praying some of those bums inside'll drop dead—that's why we're hanging around." You could see the men working in the shed, and I mean they were running their tails off. Like I said, I shouldn't have gone.

And I didn't know where else to try, either, that always makes you feel real great. Plus being hot and tired, it was the kind of day the sidewalk heaves the heat up in your face. That's when I went over to the park. I never did eat any lunch, still getting lumps from those eggs.

So I sat down on a bench, which I also shouldn't have done. This old guy next to me—there were these old geezers planked down all over the place—all he could barely do was, if he wanted to spit, he'd rock forward and let her drop between his feet. Then he'd lean back.

It was the damn heat, I guess, but I got sort of dizzy. I kept looking around, any other way except at the old guy. And I saw this spot under the bushes. Lord, it looked cool—grass—I never wanted anything like I wanted to lie down about then. You know, it scares you to get weak all of a sudden. If I'd stopped to think, I'd have known it wouldn't look too good, but I didn't feel like worrying. I just went over there and flopped. I put my face right down in the dirt where they'd been digging around the bushes—it smelled real, it sort of brought me back to facts.

I thought, I've got to get organized. Quick. Something this Norm said—did you know there's companies that won't even look at you if you're over thirty? I felt like I ought to get up and start running. How do you have time to try enough different stuff out? Not that I'm getting old yet, but what it means is, after you're thirty you *can't* try anything new, not ever. You shut up and turn your whole lousy life over to Glister. Just *be* there. And here I'd been worrying about sixty-five.

So I guess I got worked up about that—at least I know I didn't act too great. With the cop. But when he asked me for identification, it was like I was in Russia or somewhere. That's why I got sore. That's why I just asked him if there's some law says you've got to carry a permit to walk the streets.

Suppose I was Joe Nobody lying there on the grass in a town where I didn't have any friends. I'm out of a job, low on cash—would they really run me in maybe? So when he said, "Let's see your driver's license and no back talk," all I did was mention how I wasn't driving anywhere. I was trying not to get smart—Pop told me, if I ever got smart with the law I was on my own. He said, if it ever came up, I should answer their questions and never act griped.

So I was pretty reasonable about it. I told him, "I was only lying there because I looked for a job all day and I'm beat."

The cop says, "How do you expect anybody to hire you if you look like a bum, fellow?" I think he was trying to give me advice, he wasn't too shirty. And I had to admit I needed a shave even worse by then.

"Well," I said, "I guess I got dirty lying there, but I got a tie in my pocket if that'll make you happy," and I showed it to him.

He was still not too sure about me, I guess. He asks, "Are you broke, bud?" I didn't know if he was hinting for a tip or what. Some cops will take one, only with my luck I'd offer it to some guy that's the FBI in disguise and get booked for bribery. Anyhow, he was getting this look like the jailhouse is the next stop.

For a minute I thought, good, go right ahead, buster—we'll see about that. I shoved my hands in my pockets like come and get me. And then I guess I changed my mind, anyhow I pulled out my driver's license and my wallet had plenty of cash in it. I thought, take some, go ahead, help yourself if you want. Which he didn't.

He gave me a glance like, what kind of a nut are you? Naturally he saw the address, and my name's the same as my father's—Pop's pretty active around the city, so the cop probably did a take on that. He finally says, "O.K., move along."

And I moved along—what else? I didn't get violent, I don't know why he'd think I was upset. Except I noticed him tailing me about a block back, I got nervous and went the wrong way for the bus—I had to go around a couple more blocks and walk over to

Broadway again. With him dogging me—what do they expect, you to act *normal* while they're spooking around like that?

. . . .

Rion started to go on and ask it—something you ought to know, something a lawyer should be able to fill you in on.

This guy was sharp—kind of a mind reader, too. He stacked his papers back in his briefcase, then looked up and said, "What's on your mind, son?"

"I was just wondering. About bribes. Like how *do* you know when to shell out?" And all at once a lot hung on the answer. Because he knew he'd put the old boy on the spot. If he tries to shrug it off and says it's all a myth, who's he kidding? Rion thought, if your own lawyer won't level with you—

For a second, the attorney seemed to stall. Took off his horn-rims to polish them, and suddenly his face looked tougher. "Son, it's about like poker. If you want to buy in on a crooked game, then learn to stack the deck. But that kind of thing I don't teach."

Rion felt his ribs loosen up. "Yeah"—he had to laugh—"used to make Nick sore if I even asked. He says that's why they pass so many new laws every year, so more people get green pockets. He says a lot of young guys don't want to kink up, but they have to—to compete. It made him burn. I heard him tell some of the other men once, 'Watch out, though, one of these days the old mossbacks down at the courthouse are going to find out a few other kinds of laws they never heard about yet.' Like the population explosion, he meant. 'We got a smart bunch of kids growing up, they could bring on a whole new look.' It used to kill me—I thought, *damn it, I'm one of 'em!* That's what got to me, going home that day. Because when you spend your life shoving furniture around, you don't bring on anything but a colossal pain in the back. That's what I was going to try and tell Doug."

"You hadn't seen him since his blowup the night before?"

"No, Lord no. I wanted him to get over the headache, you know, before we came out for another round. And this time, I thought, I'm going to listen to him for a change. That's what was wrong with the whole deal, me not listening enough. Some of those things he said—he was right, about muscle being no proof of anything. And how that's not where you get your kicks, but—what he called it—a contest of minds. Damn right. The only thing that ever charged me really hard was when people would get all excited about some idea, like Doug used to. So he's always had the answers, he must have now. If I could just show him I want to hear about it. With all the rest on tilt, I had to keep clear with Doug. I just focused on that all the way home. . . ."

13

. . . .

So I wasn't on the prod or anything when I got there. All I decided was, the biggest foul-up had been because there was too much babe around. So if she's there this afternoon again, she'll have to stand aside and shut up. Women better learn that once in a while. The nerve of her, telling Doug a lot of stuff last night, getting him sore at me. I might even clue her in on a few things one of these days, I thought. Of course he shouldn't have *let* her sell him that stuff, either. So I guess I gave them both a look when I came in the back way and they were there in the kitchen.

Shirli seemed different somehow, she didn't give me her hand to kiss. And Doug was like one of those stone heads they carve out of a mountain.

I said, for everybody's information, "No thanks, I don't want anything to eat and I don't feel like having any cracks bounced off me, I'm only hanging in here waiting to get a word or two with my brother, who also happens to be a buddy of mine, I thought, but don't let me interrupt anything important, don't anybody bother to come down to the rec room unless you feel like it." I wasn't shirty, but it got across. Shirli, it's the first time I ever saw her look even slightly shook.

Doug tells me when he gets down in the basement—I'm putting on a stack of Tijuana Brass and like that, I kind of needed it about then—Doug says, "That was a very strange little speech you made."

"I should've started sooner," and I meant it. "Only I don't want to talk about her, you're on your own with that one. What I wanted to say is, after all that last night you got me thinking. I guess I did throw my weight around about this school thing, and you're right—I'm a dope and it bugs me, so I won't buck it any more, trying to act like I've got something going. Because the truth is, I don't." I said, "If you'll help me study up and all, I know I need to, even if it's only the crummy Institute and I don't know why I'm going there." But somehow, the more I tried to spell it out, the worse it sounded. I don't blame him for being kind of leery.

He says, absent-minded like, "What the devil are you trying to pull now?"

"For cornsake, I'm telling you—I know you've got everything figured," I said. "You always did. I never heard anything you couldn't explain, better than practically anybody else in the world."

"Are you out of your mind?" he kind of bust out. Why should he get mad? He says, "What did you hear just now when you came in? Are you taking some cue from Shirli again, with your sly jabs?"

"*Who's jabbing?*" I yelled. "*I admire you, damn it!* You always did know what you were doing, you had the right idea. Stuff like that time you were going to tackle Harlem—and it's true, now we got riots." Every time I see 'em on TV I get clinched up good inside, I wished I was raving around, belting out some songs and standing up to the fire hoses. Only I shouldn't have mentioned it to Doug.

"Who's been trying to enlist you in the Communist party?" he sort of sneers.

"What's the Commies got to do with it? I just

thought, like these demonstrations—it's what you used to say we've got to do, rally support, wake up the public and all." He did, too. He was for non-violence all over the place.

"Strictly for fanatics," he tells me now. "What the field of civil rights needs is individual moral responsibility. If you want to study to be a preacher—" He really was getting shirty, I thought. He kept looking toward upstairs, but he didn't seem in much hurry to go back there.

I said, "Well, maybe they're fanatics, but at least they're on the move. Like what about that cleanup drive you practically sold Pop on? You ever still think about that?"

"That was in my sophomore year," he says, as if that explains everything. "Anyhow, if slum clearance ever does get funded it will be wallowing in grift, I wouldn't touch it."

So—that takes care of that. I still don't get it. He thinks it's a dirty racket? Well, *naturally*—anything can snowball into a dirty racket, I thought he knew. He reads the papers, I thought the idea is to go in and buck it. Like Nick said, bring on the new look.

Anyhow, I sure wasn't playing in the right key for him—he kept memorizing the picture over the sofa, a big bunch of sloppy sunflowers. All at once I got kind of nervous. He looked like he was glazed over, on the inside where it counts. I felt like I had to shake him up. I wanted him to get excited, the way he used to—charge up and down or spin a chair around backward and slam down into it, talk a blue streak. That's all I could think of, to gig him somehow.

I said, "O.K., so you've got everything all explained and tied up and put away. You're going to be a great key personnel man, but I got news. I been digging my heels into a lot of hot concrete today— I saw some of those guys. And if anybody was never the key to anything. They look like they're skipping their whole lives, that's all. Maybe it was hokey, but you used to have ideas—like ambitions. A hell of a lot of them!"

Then I really got scared. Even that didn't get to him. He looked at me through ten feet of dead quiet and he says, "Ideas. I told her, you can't go off half-cocked about every little impulse. You can't really live on dreams. You've got to . . . buy things. It doesn't kill you to be practical," he says, and he's dying. "The ideas . . . will keep. You can always explore them, later when you have time. They'll still be there, developing in the brain cells—Phillipson says it's even better that way, to keep them there in secret and leave them alone until they come bursting to the top. Like yeast rising in hot water."

"Lukewarm," I said, I wasn't thinking, only you learn it in cooking. "Yeast only works in lukewarm." Damn, I didn't mean anything.

But all at once his chest goes to heaving, like the time down at camp when the director found our copperheads—some live ones we collected. Anyhow, he's all shook—Doug is—he says, sort of slow and gruesome, "That's—been—the size of it. All along, tearing me down. Well, old buddy, go ahead. Tell me more. About how stupid I am. Knocking my career, my whole philosophy."

I swear I didn't know he had one, even. All I could tell him, I said, "What difference? Who cares who knocks anything? If you were really turned on about personnel—except you aren't. And if you don't get a jolt, *some* kind of a blast, what good is it? You ought to *feel* something. I mean, take my heap out on the Interstate, if you want to know. Put her up to sixty, just between sixty and sixty-five—she sings."

Somehow he works his face into a smile, I guess you'd call it. "Shirli told me about your love affair with your tin lizzie. She said she was jealous. Oh, you two have had a happy time with your little by-play. Very interesting. You'll make a great case history." He's looking at me like I was upside down in a jar. "Of course you don't know what you've really done. Everything . . . ruined. And I can't even get angry—you're too unhinged to comprehend the full, total extent of it." Very slow, he says, "That's why . . . some people pull the legs off flies . . . and beat little children to death. They're unbalanced, they're no longer—human."

When he walked out of there, believe me, he was rigid.

14

. . . .

It happened so fast and quiet—I was sweating for some reason, I just knew I had to keep on the move. I turned off the record player and shoved in my shirttail, then I kind of followed my knees on out to the heap. And there she is, sitting in the front seat.

I didn't mess around with being civilized, I said, "Beat it. Right now."

She just sat. "You'll have to remove me bodily— I'm sure you're up to it."

Not that I was about to touch her—you start hauling girls around, you've really got jailhouse trouble. But I wasn't going to let her keep me from getting out of there, and I didn't want to discuss it, either.

I said, "Will you kindly get your own body out of my car, *I am not interested.*" That was crude, if Doug should ever want to know.

She just sat there, it was a little different-type act than before.

What do you do? I said, "If you go out of here with me, you might find yourself thumbing a ride home."

"I've been doing that all my life, always a hitch-hiker on some strange road." And she sinks down farther in the seat, way off to one side, so at least she's not going to climb in my lap. I wouldn't have stood for that. When I'm driving, *no* girl starts any funny stuff.

Finally I got in, but I gave it one more try. "You already loused things up between me and my brother, who is a great guy and you should live so long as to have him look at you. So why don't you crawl on back in the house instead of always being where you don't belong?"

"I'm never where I belong," she says, "but especially not in there. Doug knows it—it's all over. Poor Doug, he's safe, you can stop worrying. Tomorrow I'll be gone, you won't even remember what I look like. But for the sake of holy heaven, let's don't throw away tonight."

Only she used stronger language, I don't like to repeat it. When I cuss around, it doesn't mean anything. But girls do it, they aren't kidding. I never cared for that too much. If Doug and her were finished, I was so glad I thought—O.K., baby, hang on, you asked for it. And took off.

Maybe I shouldn't have, but I guess I didn't care a whole lot. Mainly I needed to get some air moving —get the smell of that bull session out of my head. She sure did wear good perfume, I'll say that . . . it's like I got a drift of something.

With the sun gone down and the sky cool, my head eased off. Up to then it felt like a hot potato, like you could stick it with a fork and it would shoot steam. So now a few things began to clear a little.

I could see why he was acting so walleyed down there if she just gave him the kiss-off. And me letting her tag along wasn't the best idea I ever had, he probably saw us leave. But it might help him to blow—I mean, you've got to, at somebody. Tomorrow he can call me a werewolf, you know? Then I hoped we could smooth it all out, because one thing kept coming in on me. That he really was a lot differenter than I liked to admit. Give or take one babe in pink jersey.

She was the only one who might know some of the answers, too—she was with him all this year. I asked her, "How long have you been a friend of Doug's?"

She had to think. "Once, for seven and a half minutes. When he was telling me about the greatest thing that ever happened to him."

"Which would be this Phillipson?"

"No, much earlier. When he won a debate in high school. Given: that our foreign policy should support nationalism around the world. He could still repeat his whole summation, about all the proud little countries—it was beautiful. That was before the day of Mr."—so forth and so on—"Phillipson."

I said, "What kind of a screw is he, anyway?"

"The kind," she says, "who would feel it his duty to tell you there were grasshoppers in the Chinese soup. Just as you were starting to enjoy it."

Reminded me of Mr. White. He wouldn't have touched a raw onion if you held a gun on him, I bet.

She says, "I only took his course so I could needle him. A waste of effort—you can't prick a thin stream of escaping gas. So one does the best one can—I needled Doug. I thought it might help, but I guess I've punctured him. Why does life get so complicated?"

That made me start to burn. "You were trying to *help?* When you used Mom's crystal bowl for a lot of dirty shrimp? And telling Doug all that junk about me?"

"He kept trying to analyze your guts—they worry him. You're either a paranoiac or antisocial. I'm manic-depressive myself. Manic, right now—tonight—in spades." And all at once she gets stretchy. Any time a girl goes stretching around . . .

I had to slow down, I was driving too fast. Right then I felt like I should keep going clear on to San Francisco and get on a boat. Across some ocean, out where the action is—I don't mean like with the Army, I couldn't care less. But Asia, some place where these little characters are glad to die for their crummy rice. Burning themselves up—they still care about everything. I wished I could feel like that—it was boiling around in my head. I didn't even know I was talking until Shirli picked it up.

"That's why you make Doug uncomfortable—you still have hopes. I wish you were right, oh Lord, I wish you were right! If this was the last night I was going to live," she says, "I'd like to spend it standing beside you on top of a burning building, loading the guns while you fought them off—all the cruel, torturing, ruining sons-of-—" And, like I said, she meant every word.

For some reason I couldn't seem to keep the speed from sliding up—I kept having to watch the road too close, I couldn't think. So I took a turnoff, leads to that little park—you know, the state historical monument. What's left of an old log fort up on a hill, dates back to Daniel Boone or something. I thought if Shirli wants to stand on the roof of it, don't let me stop her.

But after I get parked, she just sits there looking out at the sky. It was dark by then. "Your sign's not up yet," she says. And goes on, how he was a great hunter—this Orion. Only his girl friend did him in because he wouldn't get cozy. Oh, I could see where she was heading all right. Says this What's-her-name was goddess of the moon, "and all the wild places and wild things—mistress of the boar, the stag and the wolf. . . ."

I don't know, like I said, being out at night gives me hair on my neck. I told her, "Turn it off, will you? I've got a lot else on my mind, I got to think."

She got amused, almost. "I tried that once, but my parents frowned on it. Might make the headlines, you know, mustn't be noticeable. The invisible people—my mother and father—they can't even see each other through the rich fog around our house. So vulgar to raise one's voice, even in a song to the Almighty. Mustn't disturb anybody. And bright colors are cheap, so damn the wild yellowbells, stick to the tea roses. But especially, don't think. It might ruin your future as a lovely—young—suburban—matron."

I told her, "If that last crack was about Doug, you should be glad somebody cared about making you a nice future. That's all he was trying to do, set it up right."

"I know," she mumbles. "I know, that's why I came here. I figured you should try a thing on for size. All my dear sisters will soon be making a full-time career out of it—trotting from the electric kitchen to the League of Women Voters. But for me, there lies the future." She points to the crumbly old cabin. "I'll bet there's a graveyard behind it. Gloomy things, the graveyards of the night. I want neon on my headstone. Just one word: *Born*. Because that's the beginning of the end, and there's nothing in between worth mentioning except—" Well, what she was getting at, she begins to fiddle with her buttons. I wasn't exactly looking, but I could see her hand moving in the moonlight.

Don't tell me, I never should've got into a spot like that. But by then all I could do was keep brushing her back. I said, "You're just teed off because you're a girl, only I got news. You better settle for it. And hope you get a nice guy to be around in case the going gets rough."

"You think a woman can't fight, too? But there's

nothing worth dying for and only one thing worth living for. I could show you—" And she was about to. Right then.

All at once I thought, damn her for crowding me —I'll hunt my own game if she should ask. And damn her anyway, for being so *wrong*. There's got to be more to it than this little peanuts.

"Little cheating peanuts!" I told her. "No wonder you think there's nothing worth a flip, you're so busy going after these wormy, rotten peanuts. Peanuts that aren't even there—the old shell game, pick up the shells, somebody's palmed them all. So you got let down because Doug didn't throw pillows at you? Well, remind me to tell him sometime, the only mistake he made was thinking you wanted something big. And all you care about is cheap kicks? Baby, you don't know the score even as much as I do. You're *nowhere*."

Somehow I had to get in gear before I was nowhere, too. And everything else in the world. I just headed for the lights over on the Interstate, I needed some traffic. When I came off the inbound ramp, I shoved the heap up to seventy and made the center lane—I wanted to be right in the middle of a crazy lot of people, busting along somewhere.

Come to think, that's about when I first had to fight the car a little. The white line kept moving in on me, like it was warping. But I just thought—well, hell, I felt like I didn't breathe once until we came over the viaduct and I saw the exit coming up, NORTH SIDE.

. . . .

With the memory coming at him now like a race-way, Rion swerved to a stop.

"Problem?" the lawyer asked.

"Yeah. I got to think how to tell this next part. Because there's a certain party I wouldn't want to get in any trouble."

The briefcase got unzipped again, another paper —the attorney glanced down the sheet. "Joanna Duncan. Proprietor of the Rockaway Bar. Her statement admits you were there, she says she didn't know you were under age. It may cost her a fine, but she doesn't seem worried."

"That's Jo. Jeez, to go out on a limb for me. Well, you can tell the cops—she really doesn't know my age. I got going to her place with Fred and a couple of older guys from the doghouse. Last year, about the time Nick was sent up—she knows him, too. That's why we went there, we were trying to cheer her up, but it was mostly the other way around.

152 . . .

She'd let me sound off awhile, then she'd go get some change from the cash register and feed the jukebox. 'Come on,' she'd say, 'you can't go sour while you're shaking it up.' I shouldn't mention that, either—Jo doesn't have an entertainment license. She'd have to shove the prices up. So whenever she feels like dancing with one of the guys, somebody will go stand in the doorway and scout. . . . I shouldn't be telling this. I'd rather cut off my tongue than get Jo in any jam."

"You're not spilling too many beans," the attorney told him. "You don't think the stamp of feet goes unnoticed in the night?"

"Yeah, I guess people know about it—Jo's got a pretty firm step." For being old—maybe forty, fifty years old. Rion felt a little sick when he thought about it, she shouldn't ever be that old. The way she can dance! "She knows good music, too. You wouldn't think for somebody that has to dye their hair—I mean, she just touches it up a little, it looks good—" That was what always bugged him about older people, you could hardly be too truthful about how they look and all. The point was, she seemed so little-kid happy when she was dancing. "She runs a real clean place," he went on in a desperation. "Sort of a family-type gin mill. They better not make any trouble for her, on account of me."

15

. . . .

The trouble was, everything sprang a little loose—
when I blew my stack at Shirli, I mean. Because
what she was after was sort of the same thing I'd
been thinking—she wished she could feel something. Even if it seemed to me she was settling for
small chips, I practically felt sorry for her, the way
she sat there on the other side of the seat with her
lip buttoned crooked. I thought she could use a
drink, maybe relax her a little. She looked like if
she moved, she'd break off at the hips.

So between feeling rotten, having to ice her down that way, and worrying about my own fenders flapping, I just naturally headed for Jo's place. I needed to hear that jukebox—she's got a bunch of these old-time numbers from years back. She won't let the music-rental company touch 'em. That's one reason I hang in there sometimes, you know where you're at. And she'd never ask where I picked up a doll like Shirli.

Not Jo. She just gave me the glad sign when I walked in. Lord, when I caught a look at myself in the mirror behind the bar—I still had on the same clothes I was lying on the grass in. And you could've struck a match off the beard by then. I really looked like a bum. With Shirli in this dress that's just a pink sliver. You know how these plain clothes look like money?

I gave a quick once-around, I hoped there was nobody from the doghouse. I'd hate the guys to think I brought some babe over north slumming. Nobody except some of Jo's own regulars, but they were giving Shirli the eye, all right. I knew then it was a mistake.

"Listen," I said, "maybe we shouldn't have come in here. They don't exactly welcome girls to sit at the bar."

"Good," she says and wedges her hip onto a stool.

Jo gives me a grin and says, "Where you been keeping yourself, honey?" Like I bring in poison-pink babes in earrings all the time.

Of course, as soon as Shirli sees there's something good going between me and Jo, she begins to hitch up her socks. "What a charming place. Is this your *own* little saloon? How wonderful—to have a spot where you can really express your personality."

Jo gives me the wink. "If you're referring to the cracks in the plaster, they belonged to the previous owner. The scuffs in the floor are all mine, though. Excuse me, while I go make a few more." One of the guys was waving at her, he always dances her around to the Tennessee Waltz.

A little beer, I began to ease off inside, but not Shirli. She ordered a double shot, and all it does, when she sees Jo dancing, it makes her start to twitch.

She says to me, "Now I know how you got to be an expert on cheap kicks."

I said, "Drink it and let's go."

"You go, junior," she says, and taps her glass on the bar for more. When Jo comes, it starts again. Shirli says, "How lovely to see the quaint old dances. My parents used to do the Tennessee Waltz, it was quite touching."

Jo doesn't even flicker. "What happened to their

baby sitter tonight, Lollipop?" Which I don't blame her, she had to hold her own with all her regulars listening in. Everybody was beginning to give us looks, there wasn't a record on right then.

When Shirli finally wanders off to the powder room, I said to Jo, "Lord, I'm sorry. Only how do I get her out of here?"

"Quit buying, maybe?" But you know Shirli would have some money of her own. Then Jo gets another idea. "Or make her want to leave, take the stage away from her."

By then, Shirli's on the way back and I noticed her give a glance at some guy that just came in, sitting up at the far end of the bar. I never saw him before. Nick would've put him down for small-time, but maybe tough under the shirt. You don't wear a monogrammed silk shirt in that neighborhood unless you're ready, willing and able. The way Shirli gives a slight smile, like he's a whole new set of golf clubs—I had a hunch I should hustle her out of there before she finished that second double. But it doesn't do a bar any good to have a racket go on, and you could tell she'd make one.

Meantime Jo's fooling with the jukebox, and those first chords that came on, I knew what her play was. Because this old piece—"Whole Lot of Shakin' Going On"—I'm the only one she says can handle it the way she likes. And all the guys are calling, "Come on, kid. That's your number." She's holding out her hand, and I guess I sort of wanted to show Shirli a thing or two. Or maybe I just felt like to hell with everything. When the right music hits me . . .

And Jo does a lindy like she's on skates. I never saw anybody move so easy and right. I don't even have to look at her—I close my eyes and stick out my hand. All it takes is one touch, and she's right where I want her—anywhere, I can't explain. But every time we ever did it I lost track. The piano slamming you in the guts and the guy kind of whispering, "Shake, baby, shake"—only it's more like the beat goes through you, like a shiver. The world could fall in.

So I didn't see anything, not until the sound dies and there's Jo looking over my shoulder at what's going on up the bar. Shirli had moved over a couple of stools and is all elbowed up against this character. As I got there I heard her saying something—"Don't worry about baby brother," meaning me. I knew the guy could take me if he wanted to, but I figured it was no time to waste.

I hauled her off the seat by both elbows and headed her for the door—we nearly made it, too. We were almost out of there, even with Shirli digging her heels into my shin, when all of a sudden this character is in my way. I knew he could get around fast.

He says, "Sonny boy, that ain't even polite, to treat a lady like that."

The rest is pretty mixed up. I know I shoved the car keys in her hand and pushed her out the door. Somehow I was outside too, I guess I hauled him with me—I was thinking of Jo. He gave me a chop, I don't know if I ever did land a good one on him. But he got me once with his knee, so I grabbed him, sort of. Then he yelled something—or maybe he didn't exactly yell, but I thought he was calling to a friend of his. So when I felt somebody grab my shoulder, I turned swinging.

You'd think a cop would know better than to come up behind you when you're really wading in. And with my lousy luck, I had to connect. The minute he folded up on the sidewalk, the other guy was gone. I guess that's what he was saying while we were wrestling around—telling me to knock it off, the law was moving in. But when you get mad, you don't listen. Built up the way I was, from three or four days back, I guess I did look like I'd just as soon slug the other cop—the one who arrested me.

But I never resisted arrest, the way he claimed. I never had the chance, he got the cuffs on me too fast—they must have plenty of practice. I did jaw at him some. I think I said, "If it's against the law for a guy to protect a girl that's with him—"

Cop says, "I don't see any girl. What girl?"

Because she wasn't around. All that talk about loading the guns and women can fight, too—I wondered where that went. Or was she thinking about those headlines she mentioned? That was probably it. At least when they drove me on off to the station, we went past my car and I could see her sitting in there, all crouched over. Like she was keeping her face out of sight maybe—I don't think she could've been crying.

So if I sounded a little what they called incoherent, when they booked me—I mean you see them put all this stuff down: drunk and disorderly, disturbing the peace, assault with intent.

I said, "There was *no intent*. I was ducking a lot of knuckles."

They go ahead writing. "Resisting arrest, striking an officer." The cop with the sore jaw was there—his peace was disturbed all right. He told them in a few short words that I was definitely the one doing the swinging.

"But I'm not drunk!" I kept saying, which was always good for another laugh. And that made me burn some more, I know I was yelling around, because the desk sergeant picked up his pen and wrote something else down.

When he did that I tried to shut up a little. I told them, "Listen, call my brother. He'll explain the whole thing." By then I figured she'd be home and she and Doug could rig up whatever story they wanted, to cover the deal and still keep her out of it. Anything I said might put her on the spot and him too, and anyhow, as a liar I'm very lousy.

So I gave the desk sergeant our home phone number while they stood around—these men with their faces, their eyes were as flat as dishwater. They didn't care what I said, not a damn. Funny, I remember hearing the traffic go by outside, it must've been midnight by then. The trucks kept roaring on past like nothing at all.

At last somebody says, "O.K., lock him up." That's when I realized that up to then, I didn't believe it could really happen.

. . . .

Rion stared at the lawyer's wristwatch, a plain steel Omega that probably cost a couple of hundred. It showed ten minutes to five. "You want to knock it off for tonight?" he asked, hardly knowing whether to hope for a yes or a no.

"Let's wrap it up. Unless you're tired?"

"It's not that, but— Listen, sir, suppose I just confess: I was drunk and disorderly, the next day I thought how it would embarrass my folks, so I decided to skip town and got driving too fast and cracked up. They couldn't call me crazy for that?"

"You might beat the sanitarium, but not the jail-house."

"So—"

"Wasn't one night in the tank enough to convince you it's got no future—the big bore of this world?"

Rion couldn't even kid himself about that. "You get the message when they turn the key—you'd have to be made of concrete. Feels pretty peculiar. You're there for as long as they want to make it. Sit and watch the junkies with the shakes. I didn't know what I was supposed to do, so I sat on the floor and didn't do anything. I guess that could go on for months, huh?"

"Years."

Some optimist, this lawyer.

"Son," he said, "you've come this far with the story, why not finish it?"

"Because the worst comes last. I've been thinking, ever since last night. Mom and Pop were here—she got crying again. They don't know what it's all about, Doug and me and all. They're so mixed up."

"Which is why you've got to unmix them. They only know parts of the story—the bits and pieces the police know."

"But it's going to make them feel lousier when I tell the rest."

"And yet it's worse not to know the whole score. You understand that. And there's nobody but you to clear it up." The attorney wasn't throwing any weight—it was more like he was caught in the middle himself. "That's the trouble with having a strong sense of responsibility."

"Who, me? You got to be kidding. Don't even mention that word. I'm through with it—taking too much onto myself, I don't have the horsepower. It's why I couldn't explain to the cops about Shirli. It's the reason I figured wrong about Doug. It even got me in trouble down at that camp."

"And that's another thing. Even though it's a far cry from city jail to the Silver Wolf pack, I wish you'd take time out right now to set the record straight on that camp business."

"How'd you know that was the name of my squad of kids?"

"The truth is—one of the questions that have been raised regarding the stability of your mental health is how you got into that mess. The director has made a statement about your dismissal. He says the paths around the camp are well marked. The trails, you couldn't miss if you were blind. Anybody who *could* get lost there would have to be, he says, an idiot."

Coming up off the pillows, Rion felt the hard jab of anger—it was a relief, as if a boil had been pricked and pricked good. All of them, the whole bunch, so ready to jump to their stupid conclusions.

"So he says, did he? I never even knew he was in on this. You'd think he might maybe come ask me a few private questions before he gives out any remarks. Or he could've listened to me that night— I was trying to explain. Well, damn, if he's going to go around saying I'm a nut—here I've been trying not to knock his camp, just because he hired me once. That's how jackass I can get! All right, I'll tell you, and there wasn't anything idiot about it."

16
· · · · · · · · · ·

It's not so far off the subject of the clink, either. The guy runs the place like a concentration camp. Or maybe a zoo, only backwards. He practically puts the kids in a cage for fear they'll get hurt and their parents will sue him. What does he care if the kids hate it? I did too—I felt the same way, like kicking around at the dust every time the coordinator blew his whistle. So that day after the director killed our snakes—

That's what slays you about kids. They loved

those crummy snakes. I only started out to show them how to handle a real dangerous snake, so they'd be careful. But they had to keep the things and feed them and name them. So when the guy smashes them, the whole squad was just about sunk. But you should see how they cooled it—walked away like they couldn't care less. When they could've bawled just as easy—I guess that's what got me, they're so gutty.

Come afternoon, I was supposed to lead them on this nature walk, and boy, if there was one thing we didn't give a hang about, it was looking at the same initials carved all over the same trees. They wanted to play baseball, they kept asking me, "How do I pick a man off first?" And they'd say, "Tell us again how you struck out eleven guys in the play-offs." I don't know, it just came home to me—how I was their counselor, me, I was the leader. I was supposed to do something for them. And here we'd been just killing time for weeks.

Anyhow I noticed how some of them kept inching out from the path—which you were told: don't ever do. Those woods down there really are dense. But the kids would keep drifting a little, like they were testing me.

I said, "None of that stuff. If we're going to break trail into new territory, we're going to do it right, all together." The way they took off, you'd have thought I said check in at the Canadian border by sundown.

I had to get tough with them before we got all organized. I told them we had to stick close, and I showed them how to blaze trees. At first I didn't figure we'd go too far—you couldn't see very deep in those woods at all. And I was about to turn around and find my way back out while there was still plenty of light, when I suddenly thought, the hell I will!

The way I figured it, they ought to learn how to get lost while there's somebody around. I even wanted to try it myself. How else do you know what you'll do? These things on survival always bugged me—you wonder if you could make it. I even thought I could explain that to the camp director tomorrow, how it was good for us.

Worked out very easy—to get lost did. All I did was quit blazing the trees. As soon as I told 'em I had no idea where we were, man, were they happy. Scared out of their pants. They all began to eat— those kids always carried some kind of goop in their pockets. So they ate like they were maybe going to starve to death the next ten minutes.

They wanted to climb the tree with me, only I wouldn't let them. I think they were wishing I'd see the camp and yet hoping I wouldn't, too. So, like I told them, nothing but more treetops.

That kind of made them get serious. They closed in on me, a little nervous, hollering how they were hungry and all that. It was the only tight spot in the whole deal. But I got out of it, I said, "Well, why the hell didn't you watch the way we came? You all got knives, why weren't *you* blazing the trail? Who ever guaranteed you that the counselor couldn't get lost?"

That really set them up. They felt great—like they had this suspicion all along there was something fishy about counselors. About then one of them runs up with this frog he just caught. He says, "This is what *I'm* going to eat." I got to admit my stomach flipped a little, but not those kids. They *all* wanted a frog.

When I made a fire in this little clearing, two or three of them went and made their own fires. Man, I was proud of them, they must've been watching how I did it. Anyhow, I thought, they're sure not playing baby games like being a Silver Wolf tonight. And when they went to make their beds out of grass and stuff, it's the first time they ever really listened to what poison ivy was.

I don't know . . . after they quieted down and I was sitting there alone, I was feeling no pain. Not even the frog leg I ate. I kept thinking how, for a counselor, I sure got them unoriented. But I couldn't see it was such a bad thing. You know, you're always part of something—your family or school or a team. I had this idea it was good to feel separate for a while, figure where you're at. And it would feel real great to them tomorrow when we worked it out, how to find our way back. We could get our directions when the sun came up—I was just beginning to get this firm feeling. . . .

Then the highway patrol chopper came. Oh, I guess I knew they'd have to send out a fool search. And as soon as he spotted our fires, he dropped a flare to show the ground party where we were. Lord, I wished he didn't do that—it just hung up there over us, this ugly red light, muddying everything up. The kids were jumping around like a lot of nubby little red monkeys. I shouldn't blame them for being glad to get rescued—they're only little. But it made me sick.

I felt sort of the same way that night in the tank. All these winos lying around, sleeping it off—I got this feeling the red light just went off up there somewhere and I was clobbered.

17

· · · · · · · · · ·

No point in trying to shrug it off, it's no barrel of
kicks—to be locked up. Back inside, there aren't
any windows, you can't even tell if it's getting to be
nearly morning. You think the dumbest stuff—like,
what if a fire broke out or the building falls in? You
feel like some kind of animal.

I nearly raised a racket just so the guard would
come back and chew me out, I'd feel more human.
I wished I could get sore again—it braces you some.
Only the more I thought, there wasn't anything to
get sore at. You couldn't blame the cops. Not even

the guy who ran off—he was doing what came naturally. And Shirli wouldn't have been on the scene at all if I didn't take her there.

Only I guess what I really kept thinking, one hour and then another hour—I wondered where on the green earth was Doug?

He must be all smoked up about the deal—she wouldn't tell him how it really happened. But he can figure things for himself, and he knew me longer than he did her. I hoped his radar was working. Or else what *was* taking him so long?

They'd given us some slop to eat and let some of the drunks out, so I knew it must be morning. But me they just kept looking at, this very odd way. Couple of plainclothes guys came back there— they'd sort of stroll past the cell like they were counting the house, but what they were doing was looking at me.

Finally I asked one if I could make a telephone call. He said, didn't I make one last night? And I said, no, I didn't, I thought they were supposed to let you make one.

So he says, well, a call was made, wait a minute he'll go check on it. And that was all, he didn't come back. That really did get me worried. There was only one place they'd have known to call, which was home.

Finally another bird came—Lord knows who he

was, he came right on in the tank with the guard watching at the door and he starts taking my pulse like I was sick. He said, "How do you feel this morning?" They never did that to any of the drunks.

I said, "O.K." I didn't get it.

He says, "How much do you remember about last night?"

Which I told him, I remember every bit of it, and I gave him the rundown again. He looks puzzled as if I've got some curious disease he can't figure out.

"Come along, then," he says, and we go on out to the desk.

Naturally I was looking for Doug, so when I saw Jo, I hardly realized why she was there until she gives me the old "hang tough" sign. And it dawns on me that *she's* bailing me out.

This bird that's been asking the questions says to the desk sergeant, "Same story." Like it was a miracle.

I said, "What's this all about, if you don't mind me asking? I gave you the honest goods last night—the guy attacked me, I was trying to keep from being slugged. I'm sorry I hit that police officer, but it was an accident. So what's the big problem, maybe I could help?"

They act like I didn't say anything. The plainclothes guy says, "Well, there *was* a girl, that's one thing we're sure of, so maybe the brother is protecting someone from publicity. It's an outside chance."

And they look at this character who took my pulse. He says, "I find nothing serious, and there's no record of prior commitment—I'd say we let him go, pending investigation."

I'm standing there like part of the furniture, I didn't get it at all. Then they give me my wallet back and this paper to sign and it's over—so quick, I hardly knew I was free until we were out on the street, Jo and me. She had her car parked—I didn't ask where she was driving. I just sat there, trying to get used to it—being out again.

I did try to thank her, but you can't thank people like Jo. Riding along beside her, I kept noticing little stuff like the NO TURN signs and the ONE WAY STREET markers—I felt sort of rocky for some reason.

Jo says, "You look like you could use some coffee. How'd you like to come back to my place and clean up?"

It sounded like the only thing I could face right then. I told her, "It sure was a surprise to see you. I thought Doug would spring me—that's my brother."

She didn't say anything, which is funny for Jo— she usually talks along like a telephone. But she seemed kind of sore about something. Her hair was pinned back neat, I remember. She usually lets it go loose at the bar and you can see where it's gray at the roots. I mean it's nice—makes her seem real comfortable. She was different at 10 A.M., she looked strong enough to crack somebody's head. Not mine, though.

She says, "I just called this morning to make sure somebody bailed you out, only they hadn't." She was really cussing mad about something.

I told her, "Well, they would've except my parents aren't in town right now. And Doug—it was his girl I had in the bar last night. I guess he had his hands full when she got home."

Jo gives me a look. "He told the police he didn't have a girl friend, he never heard of her. He said you couldn't possibly have been out with some girl friend of his."

I kind of got the drift of that from the way the police were talking. "He must've been trying to keep her name out of the papers. Her family's very touchy. He probably didn't realize he was lousing me up," I told Jo. "No wonder those cops looked at me like I was crazy."

She didn't say any more. We were at her apartment by then, and I went on and cleaned up. She keeps a regular man-type razor, it was very handy.

And it felt good to get a bath. When I came out, she had some coffee and orange juice and toast fixed, but I couldn't eat anything. All I could barely do was get some coffee down, I was starting to feel pretty screwed up inside about Doug.

I kept not wanting to think about it, so I tried to talk along. Like, "Nice apartment you got." It wasn't really—full of this kind of cheap furniture that you see knocked down to $59.00 at the sales. I guess she was saving her money—how did I know that, something she said?

Yeah, it was when I noticed the picture of Nick on the end table. Must've been from when he was a lot younger. I said, "What do you hear from him these days?"

And she says, "Not much. So what's new in the pen, you know?"

"I know," I said.

And she sort of looked at me, like should she or shouldn't she? All at once she said, "I bet Nick never told you—him and me were going to get married. For about ten years now. We almost made it once, we had five thousand bucks socked away, we were going to get out of here. Some good place to live— I wanted New Orleans and he wanted Vegas." She was smiling along like it was kind of a joke. "Then he blew the whole roll one night in a game. Lasted ten hours, he enjoyed every minute of it—right up to when somebody had three queens and jacks to go with 'em. 'Water under the bridge,' he says. I says, 'Yeah, there goes Niagara Falls.' But since then, I've been saving for my own old age." She was trying to get something across to me—but she kept smiling.

I didn't know how to take it exactly, I was feeling so foggy.

"I shouldn't mention anything about Nick," she goes on. "I don't usually. But he always thought so much of you—more than any of the other kids. So he wouldn't mind—he'd even agree with me, you should get as far from the north side as you can go. On out into the rest of the world, so you can judge for yourself."

"Judge—like what?" I asked.

"Everything. Like what's worth and what isn't. I mean you take Nick," she says. "You think he's a real great guy. And believe me, he is. Only what good is it doing?"

About then all I wanted was to make it as far as home, and the rest of the world could wait. I told her, "Thanks, for everything, and you're probably right, only I better get going now. My brother's got to be worrying." But what I meant was, I was worried about him. Even if it took him all night to settle up with the babe, why didn't he show this morning?

Jo's finished smiling by then. She says, "Honey, I guess I've got to tell you—maybe I should mind my own apples, but I can't let you walk in on that deal with half the deck missing. The only reason you're loose right now is because I told the fellows at the station the whole picture—girl and all. When I got there this morning and they said your story sounded cagey, I could see you were trying not to get me and the bar involved. But comes a time not to worry about that. So I explained it to them—those boys know me, they know I level. Even so, they darned near didn't let you go."

I could see she was getting mad again. Finally she comes out with it.

"Because your brother, this brother of yours, they talked to him last night. And he told them you belonged in a mental ward, he wanted them to commit you to City Hospital for observation. And they were just about to do it when I showed up."

18

· · · · · · · · · ·

I don't know, I lay there—she let me have her bed-
room to lie down, I was so tired. I thought I had to
get some sleep or something, but I was sort of
sprung wide-open inside. Like I wasn't ever going to
sleep again. My belly ached, but I could hardly feel
it.

I don't think I did sleep, but I'm not sure. Because
I only half remember Jo leaving for work. She said,
"Take it easy," or something. And I don't remember
it getting to be night—all of a sudden it was dark.

Not that I woke up exactly, I just knew it was dark. And I'd had it.

Not something I thought; it was happening and I couldn't stop it. When I wrote the check out for Jo, it was like somebody telling me how to do it. How they don't give the bail money back if a guy skips, and I wasn't going to leave her holding any bag.

I even remember my account after I got through making out the check. It was eleven dollars and twenty-seven cents. I thought, boy, with that I could buy one whole shirt like they wear in college. Or I could buy about three pair of Argyles like Norm Ashburn had on that night. Or I could buy Shirli a bus ticket halfway to Pine Bluff, Arkansas—maybe farther. Or I could buy two hundred picture postcards of Alaska.

All the way along, I kept sort of talking to myself—going home on the bus, I mean. There was nobody aboard except me, by the time we got out to our neighborhood. The driver kept whistling this old tune, and I was sort of singing along inside—you know those words? "Down and down I go, round and round I go." I got the feeling I wanted to laugh it up—best damn words anybody ever wrote in a song.

I knew it was no good, to want to laugh like that. So I talked to myself a little out loud—it didn't even seem odd. I was way at the back of the bus, I said, "Old buddy, you start to giggle around and they really will holler for the men in white." All the same, everything kept seeming like a joke. I didn't want to know if it was or if it wasn't, or why or anything.

In fact I was going to take a quiet look in the garage, and if she did bring the heap home, I hoped she left the keys in it. For a while I argued about that—would she likely do it, or would she louse things up and take the keys in the house? If she did, I was going to have to go looking, and I didn't want to think what that might lead to.

I was too cold to think. I was practically freezing, even with it being a hot night and all. I thought, if I do have to go inside, I'm going to have me a shot. But then I thought, better not, I'm going to hit that road pretty fast. And I wasn't feeling too sharp— the driver had to yell at me it was the end of the line.

All the way walking down our block I kept saying, "Cool it, cool it." But I was so chilled off inside, that made me want to laugh some more. I had to think pretty quick about something else. I thought about Jo—about her and Nick. If it was him walking along here, he'd be ready.

And then I thought, what do you mean ready? How?

When the lights were off in the house, it made me feel a little more solid. I even had sense to figure maybe it would be an idea to pack a couple of things. I stopped under the streetlight out front and counted my cash—enough to buy gas to Denver maybe, or somewhere. So I went around back and checked to make sure the heap was there. The keys were in it, O.K., so I went on up.

When I turned on the light in the hall, the flowers were stuffed upside down in the wastebasket like they'd been jammed there by a hydraulic press. So I thought, well, that's that. And I went on upstairs—I swear the house felt empty. Until I switched on the light in my room.

And he was sitting there—in my chair, over by the desk. He must've heard me coming, but he didn't call out or turn on a light. He waited for me to. That's when everything bust loose completely inside me—of all the sneaky ways to act!

He smiled this very odd smile. "I knew you'd get away from them." Like I'd escaped or something.

"Yeah, sure," I told him. "They put their brain-testing machine on me and said I had the best damn head they ever saw. Just thought you'd like to know."

He looked like he half believed me. "I'm glad they let you out."

And that really made me burn. I told him, "Just lucky I got friends, the kind that don't crawl away when somebody's put you on the spot. Or didn't you know that your little doll—who doesn't exist—this imaginary little witch that's been flirting her tail around here for a week—didn't she tell you she got me fouled up last night? How it was her fault I landed in the lockup?"

"Let's hear your version," he said, doing me a big favor. Only somehow it rang wrong—I think, now, he must have been all shook inside and was covering up.

But right then all I wanted was to pull on a clean shirt. I told him I'm not interested in filling him in on a thing. He was way out of my class—he could figure it all for himself. And I began to flip stuff in my suitcase, anything I thought I could hock.

"What do you think you're doing?" he asked, still in this peculiar high voice.

I said, "Minding my own business forever."

By then he was up, standing over me like he wanted to snatch the things back out of my suitcase. If he touched a thing I was ready to clip him, I was so sore.

"But I've got to know where you're going," he kind of pleads. "I'm responsible for you!"

"*Like—hell—you—are!*" I said. "You just keep the fire going under your own kettle of kittens, you'll have a full-time job. When you get through explaining to the folks about this spook you *don't* have for a girl friend, they'll be too mixed up to even ask about me. Then if you run out of that, you go on and explain your big plans to them, how you're going to be vice-president of something when you finish school—if you ever do. And what the whole thing's worth to you and why. And what you'll get out of it—maybe be Norm Ashburn's boss someday. That'll make you feel like you really carved out an empire! And when you get through with all that, tell 'em how your inner factors are doing, and your theories about guys that tear up flies for kicks—and how that fits in with guys who tell the cops their brother is a nut."

That's when he hit me. I saw him swing—I just wish he'd landed a good one, I needed it. But I hardly felt it, it didn't even rock me. He had no weight behind it, damn him—if he'd really slugged me then, maybe it would've been all right. But he knew he'd pulled the punch. He sort of hung there with his mouth open, like he'd just seen somebody die. I—I couldn't help him. I couldn't do a thing, could I? What could I do?

I slammed the suitcase closed and somehow I was

in my car. I don't even know how long it was afterward or where I was going or anything, when I found myself fighting the road. I only knew I couldn't make it, I was going too fast—it was too late.

．．．．．．．．．

It was two weeks later that the lawyer's secretary ushered Rion into the inner office. He stood hesitant just inside the door, hands shoved in the pockets of his jeans. Now that he was on his feet again, the component parts seemed tighter, the angles were under control. "I just dropped by to say thanks, sir."

"Glad you did, son." The attorney got up and shoved a chair closer to the desk. "Sit down a minute, if you have time. I take it you're on the move— your parents have been phoning me frantically. They found the note you left."

"I guess I chickened. After it all came out O.K. yesterday, they were so happy you got the charges dismissed, I couldn't bear to tell them. I mean how I can't stick around at home. They think everything's like always again, now you convinced them I'm not out of my skull." He dug up a smile, but there was no mileage in it.

The attorney nodded, as if in agreement to some unspoken thought. "How's Doug taking it? I hoped he'd be at the hearing—that written statement of his certainly helped. It bore out everything you told me, took full blame for your being in a state of semi-shock when you drove off that night. I wish I could show it to you, but when it came in the mail it was marked 'Confidential.'"

"Yeah," Rion said softly. "Must've taken some guts for him to spill the whole thing like that. I was going to thank him, but last night when we got home, he didn't come out of his room. I guess he'd just as soon not see me. All I was going to do was tell him—you know—it's O.K. Well, I'll try to put that in a letter, one of these days." Rion managed a shrug and a smile of sorts. "Ought to drop a note to the patrolman, too. For forgetting that lump on his jaw—real great. I'll do it, only right now I need to hit the road."

"Can't say I blame you. And neither do your parents, really—at least they're trying to understand. Mainly they wonder how you're fixed for cash and where you're heading. They care about you a great deal, Rion."

"Yeah, I guess. I mean, I don't know—how could they not trust somebody as much as they didn't want to believe me? But it's not their fault, I don't blame them. I'll let them know when I get somewhere—that's a promise."

"Meanwhile, if you don't want to accept their money, how about a small loan?" The attorney reached for a drawer in his desk, but Rion shook his head quickly.

"Thanks. That's—that's nice of you, only I'll make out. I feel pretty good—my ribs do. Wherever I land, I'll find some kind of job. If I get too hungry maybe I'll catch a few frogs. But to stick around here and try to play it safe—like I told them in the note, count me out. Count me gone. I'll be O.K."

"I've an idea you will. If you don't end up on some north side—I still doubt you'll find the answers there."

"It's worse when you don't know the questions. But don't worry, I'm not ready yet to settle for cheap. I want more than Saturday night and a few hands of penny ante. If I could only see some little type thing get done—one lousy old rule changed.

Like the one where you're still supposed to be a thumb-sucking infant when you're over eighteen. Somebody's got to make a dent in it, so a few people like me would get clued in before it's too late. Maybe I'll get back to the books someday, but if I do, I'll be buying the deal myself. I'll figure it out, why I'm there, and it will be up to them: If they can fill me in on what I need to know, here's the tuition. But if they're going to gas around for years and get nowhere except to mix me up, forget it. There's other ways to get ahead. Or places where I could fit—there must be some place."